Hot Greek Docs

They're supersexy and *they're single—*
but not for much longer!

Theo, Deakin, Ares and Christos have vowed
never to surrender their freedom by putting a ring
on it—but who'd have thought it would literally
take an earthquake to change their minds?

While these gorgeous Greeks are busy saving
the islanders of Mythelios after the quake,
they can't avoid the four equally dedicated women
who are right by their sides…day *and* night!

Find out what happens in:

One Night with Dr. Nikolaides by Annie O'Neil
Tempted by Dr. Patera by Tina Beckett

Available now!

Back in Dr. Xenakis' Arms by Amalie Berlin
A Date with Dr. Moustakas by Amy Ruttan

Available July 2018!

Dear Reader,

Ever had a group of pals you loved doing things with and wanted to do them again and again? Well, that's happened to me with the wonderful Amalie Berlin, Amy Ruttan and Tina Beckett. We had such a blast writing Hot Latin Docs we've decided to wing our way across the world and write about some sexy, brooding, fabulously rich Greek doctors. And it has been an absolute hoot.

I hope you enjoy the adventure as much as we did.

And remember, I love hearing feedback from readers (the good, the bad…but maybe not the ugly :)). You can follow me on Twitter, @AnnieONeilBooks, or through my website email, annie@annieoneilbooks.com.

Enjoy!

Annie O'

ONE NIGHT WITH
DR. NIKOLAIDES

———

ANNIE O'NEIL

◆ HARLEQUIN® MEDICAL ROMANCE™

**Recycling programs
for this product may
not exist in your area.**

ISBN-13: 978-1-335-66354-2

One Night with Dr. Nikolaides

First North American Publication 2018

HARLEQUIN®

TM www.Harlequin.com

Printed in U.S.A.

Visit the Author Profile page
at Harlequin.com for more titles.

This book is dedicated, for the roller-coaster
ride of creativity, to Amalie, Amy and Tina.
You're all amazing.
xx A

**Praise for
Annie O'Neil**

CHAPTER ONE

THEO'S EYES FOLLOWED the wheeled supplies trolley as it rolled past the exam bed. The moan and creak of concrete against steel shot his senses to high alert.

When his fingers were unable to gain purchase on the delicate needle he'd been reaching for he knew what was happening.

"Up you come!" He pulled the little boy he'd been treating from the exam table to his chest, careful to mind his freshly sutured knee. "You too." He beckoned for the boy's mother to stand in the doorframe, grateful for the modern reinforced framework they'd insisted on for the clinic.

She stood frozen with fear. Pragmatism demanded he pull her close to him, certain it was the safest place to be. Earthquakes weren't common in the Greek islands, but the archipelago had been subject to more than its fair share over the past few years.

"I know it's frightening, but you must stay here!" He held the terrified mother, a young woman he'd gone to school with, close to him. "Alida, please."

He tightened his grip, fighting the urge to cough as the shift and strain of drywall released chalky clouds of gypsum into the air.

"The clinic is the safest place to be."

His voice ended up sounding harsher than he'd intended. Harsh for the voice of a school-friend and a doctor. But the clinic had never borne the test of an actual earthquake, and as the seconds ground and rasped into minutes he knew the uncompromising deal he'd made with his father had been the right one. Pride for money.

An infinitesimal wince crossed his face as he remembered the handshake that had sealed his fate.

"What is happening?"

He held the pair of them tight, the toddler clinging to his shoulders, soft whimpers of fear vibrating along his small chest into Theo's.

Alida tried to take her son and run. A natural instinct, he presumed. To care. Protect. Put one's own life on the line to save that of your child.

His lips thinned. That wasn't a childhood

he'd known. And what had followed in its wake wasn't worth thinking about. Not anymore.

Waves splashed up against the back of the clinic…the secure dock had been rendered invisible. The normal gentle hum and buzz of the clinic had been replaced by a cacophony of tightly issued instructions. Phones. Alarms.

Theo lifted his eyes to the invisible heavens in thanks for the emergency training they'd insisted upon for all the staff. He and his "brothers" had never wanted anyone to feel any unnecessary pain or fear when they entered the doors of the Mythelios Free Clinic. The Malakas of Mythelios. His best friends. The closest thing he had to a real family after his own had proved to be nothing more than a mirage.

He'd get on the phone to them as soon as possible. His gut told him that whatever was happening beyond these sheltered walls would demand all of them this time. If he could even track them down…

Ares was usually in the world's latest hellhole, doing his best to put a dent in its need for medical care. Deakin's specialist burn treatment skills were in demand worldwide. Heaven knew where *he* was now. And Chris, a neurosurgeon, could usually be found in New York

City. If he wanted to be found, that was. More often than not he didn't.

Not that it had stopped him from posing for that insane calendar of local island men that had been organized to raise funds for the clinic. *Ooopaa!* Theo's eyes followed that very calendar's trajectory across the room as it slid to the floor behind the reception desk. It was his month anyway. No great loss.

Again Alida tried to pull her son away from him and run. "It's gone on too long!"

"It's nearly over now," he soothed. *As if he knew.* Earthquakes could last for seconds or minutes. There'd been tremors on the island before, but nothing like this. The Richter scale would be near to double digits. Of that he had no doubt.

He tuned in to the chaos, breaking it down and putting it back together into some sort of comprehensible order. Rattling. Sharp cries of concern. Sensory discord.

As much as Alida struggled against him, pleaded with him to free her and let her run from the building, Theo's instinct was to stay put and work through it. These were *his* patients. *His* clinic. He'd promised them solace and care from the moment they entered the bougainvillea-laced doors and he'd meant it with every pore in his body.

The need to launch into action, preparing for the storm bound to follow in the earthquake's wake, crackled through his body like electricity. It was likely only seconds had passed—a minute or two at most—but each moment had shaken the island to its core.

He heard a woman cry out in pain.

"Get in a doorway!" he shouted, his broad hands cupping the child and Alida's heads.

Not being able to control what was happening made Theo want to roar with frustration.

"Is it over?" Alida's voice was barely audible amidst the rising chaos of human voices.

Theo shook his head, tightening his grip so that she didn't leave until he was positive it was safe.

How soon were aftershocks? Immediate? The next day?

This was the cruelty of nature. You simply didn't know.

The same way you didn't know if the parents who gave birth to you would act like Alida—protectively—or like his—abandoning him at the first opportunity.

He shook his head clear of the thought. They didn't deserve one second of his attention. The people here did. The people he'd vowed to care for.

He shouted out a few instructions. Their

clinic was a small one, but there must be at least fifty people there. Doctors, nurses, patients, a few older patients who needed more care in the overnight wards.

Another crash of waves and the howl of the earth fighting against the manmade buildings upon her surface filled his senses.

Please let the clinic be spared.

He tightened his grip on the mother and child, wondering for just an instant what it would be like to hold his own wife and child. What lengths would he go to for them?

Another tremor gripped the ground beneath them.

All thoughts other than survival left him.

Theós. Let us be spared.

CHAPTER TWO

FOLD, FOLD AND TUCK.

Just the way her mother had taught her.

Perfect.

Cailey gave a satisfied grin at her swaddling handiwork, popped a kiss onto her finger, then onto the baby's nose, all the while imagining her mum giving her a congratulatory smothering hug before pulling out a huge plate of *souvlaki* for them to share. Or *bougatsa*. Or whatever it was she had magicked up in her tiny, tiny kitchen. Miracles, usually.

She ran her finger along the infant's face. "Look at you, little *mou*. So perfect. You've got your entire life to look forward to. No Greek bad boys breaking your heart. That's my lesson to you. No Greeks."

"Are you trying to brainwash the babies again, Cailey?"

Cailey looked across, surprised she hadn't even noticed that her colleague Emily had entered the nursery. The more time she spent with the babies, the more she was getting lost in cloud cuckoo land!

"Yes." She grinned mischievously, then turned to the baby to advise her soberly, "No Greeks. And no doctors."

"Hey!" Emily playfully elbowed her in the ribs. "I've just started dating a doctor, and I won't mind admitting it's a very welcome step up in the world."

Wrong answer!

"And what, exactly, is wrong with being a nurse?"

"Not a thing, little Miss Paranoid."

Emily's arched eyebrows and narrowed eyes made her squirm.

"Looks like *someone's* had her heart broken by a doctor. A Greek doctor, to be precise."

"Pffft."

Emily laughed. "All the proof I needed."

She moved to one of the cots and picked up an infant who was fussing.

"C'mon. Out with it. Who was the big, bad Greek doctor who broke our lovely Cailey's heart?"

"No one."

Someone.

"Liar." Emily laughed again.

She shrugged as casually as she could. Maybe

she was a liar, but leaving her small town, small island, and archaically minded country behind for the bright lights of London had been for one purpose and one purpose only—to forget a very green-eyed, chestnut-haired Adonis who would, for the purposes of this particular conversation, remain anonymous.

Cailey lifted the freshly swaddled infant, all cozy in her striped pink blanket, and nuzzled up close to her. *Mmm. New baby smell.*

Life as a maternity nurse was amazing, but rather than mute her urges to hold a child of her own it had only set the sirens on full blast.

Twenty-seven wasn't *that* old in the greater scheme of things. And Theo wasn't the only man in the universe. Definitely not *her* man. So...

"Cailey?"

The charge nurse...what was her name again? Molly? Kate...? Heidi? There had been so many new names and faces to learn since she'd started at this premier maternity hospital she'd become a bit dizzy with trying to remember them all... She ran through the names in her mind again...

High on the hill was the highest nurse... Heidi!

She squinted at her boss's name tag.

Heidi.

Ha! Excellent. The memory games she'd been playing were paying off. She knew she'd battle her dyslexia one way or another. She'd done enough to get this far in her medical career, though it would never take the sting out of the fact that she'd most likely never become the doctor she'd always dreamt of being.

"Sorry to interrupt, love, but I think you might want to see this."

Cailey gave the infant—Beatrice Chrysanthemum, according to her name card—a final nuzzle before settling her back into the tiny bassinet and following Heidi along to the staffroom, where a television was playing on a stand in the corner of the room.

It was a news channel. The ticker tape at the bottom of the screen was rolling with numbers…casualties? Cailey's eyes flicked back up to the main news story. There were familiar-looking buildings—but not as she was used to seeing them.

Out of the corner of her eye she saw Emily walk in, reach for the remote and turn up the volume. At first the English words and the images of a Greece she didn't quite recognize wouldn't register. They were a series of disconnected phrases and pictures that weren't falling into place.

"Isn't that the island you're from?" Emma prompted. "Mythelios?"

Cailey nodded in slow motion as everything began falling into place.

An earthquake. Fatalities. Ongoing rescue efforts.

Her heart stopped still. The pictures of devastation had switched to a live interview being conducted outside the clinic in the fading daylight.

Of course it was him. Who else could command the world's attention?

There, front and center, more breathtakingly gorgeous than she'd allowed herself to remember, was Dr. Theo Nikolaides, appealing for any and all medical personnel who could help to come to Greece in its time of need.

She tried not to morph his entreaty for help into an arrogant call for "the little people" to come and do the dirty work while he took the glory. This was a crisis and all hands were helping hands—not rich or poor, just hands.

She stared at her own hands…her fingers so accustomed to work…

"Cailey?" Heidi touched her arm. "Are you all right?"

She turned her hands back and forth in the afternoon light as the news sank in. People were hurt. Her mother could be hurt. Her brothers…

A flame lit in her chest. One she knew wouldn't abate until she was on a plane home.

No matter how much she hated Theo, hated the wounds his words had etched into her psyche, she would have to go home. Islanders helped one another—no matter what.

"I'm fine. But my island isn't. I'm afraid I'm going to need some time off."

CHAPTER THREE

IT WAS ALL Cailey could do not to jump off the ferry and swim to shore. Flights to the island had been canceled because of earthquake damage to the runway, but it hadn't put her off coming. The same way a childhood crush gone epically wrong wouldn't stop her from helping. Not when her fellow islanders needed her. And this time she would be able to do more than help with the clean-up.

Ducking out of the wind, she pulled her mobile out of her pocket and dialed the familiar number. She wanted to hit the ground running—literally—but if her mother found out she'd come back and hadn't checked in first it would be delicious slices of guilt pie from here on out.

"Mama?"

Static crackled through the handset. She strained to listen through the roar of the ferry's engine's.

"…seen Theo?" her mother asked.

Theo?

Why was her mother asking about *him*? She'd come back to the island to *help*, not answer questions about her teenage crush. Surely ten years meant she'd moved on enough in her life for people to stop asking if her heart had mended yet?

"Mama. If you're all right…" she parsed out the words slowly "…I'll go straight to the clinic."

"Go…clinic… Theo…love…brothers…getting by…"

Cailey held out the handset and stared at it. She'd spoken briefly to her mum before she'd boarded her flight last night, so she knew her brothers were unhurt and, of course, already out working. As was her mother who—surprise, surprise—had already gathered a brigade of women to feed the rescue crews and survivors at the local *taverna*.

A Greek mother, she'd reminded Cailey time and again, was nothing if not a provider of food in times of crisis.

But…*love* and *Theo* in the same sentence?

Had her mother gone completely mad or was the dodgy reception playing havoc with her sanity?

"See you soon, Mama. I love you," she

shouted into the phone, before ending the call and adding grumpily, "But not Theo!"

She glared at the handset before giving it an apologetic pat. It wasn't its fault that everyone on Mythelios was trapped in a time warp. But she'd moved on, and working at the clinic was as good a time as any to prove it.

She moved back out to the ferry's deck and squinted, trying to make out the details of the small harbor she'd once known like the back of her hand. By the looks of all the blinking lights—blue, red, yellow—it was little more than a construction site. Deconstruction, more like, she thought, grimly stuffing the phone in her bag and shouldering her backpack.

The news footage she'd seen at the ferry terminal in Athens had painted a pretty vivid picture. Some people's lives would never be the same. Two tourists had already been declared dead. Scores injured. And the numbers were only expected to rise as rescue efforts continued.

The second the boat hit the shoreline Cailey cinched the straps on the backpack she'd so angrily stuffed with clothes she'd hoped would suit the British climate all those years ago, and took off at a jog.

Some buildings looked untouched, whilst others were piles of rubble. There was a fevered, intense buzz of work as the dust-covered people of Mythelios painstakingly picked apart the raw materials of the lives they had been living just twenty-four hours earlier. Window frames. Cinder blocks. Stone. It was clear the earthquake had been indiscriminate, and in some cases brutal.

"Cailey!"

She stopped and turned. Only three voices in the world made her feel safe, and this was one of them.

Kyros!

Before she had a chance to give voice to her big brother's name she was being picked up and swirled around.

"Cailey *mou*! My little starfish! How are you?"

Despite the gravity of the situation, Cailey laughed. She never would have believed hearing her childhood nickname would feel so good. Or simply *smelling* the island, her brother's dusty chest and, miraculously, the scent of baking bread.

Together she and her brother looked across the street to the bakery. All that was left was the building's huge and ancient stone-built ovens. And there, undeterred by the open-air setting, was Mythelios's top baker, pulling loaves out as if working amidst rubble was the most normal thing on earth.

Cailey's brother smiled down on her. "I'm so glad I saw you. We're just about to go up to the mountains—see what we can do up there to help the more isolated houses." He squeezed her tight. "How is the family success story? Does that London hospital know how lucky it is to have you? Have you seen Theo?"

Cailey did her best not to let her smile falter as Kyros held her at arm's length and waited for answers. What *was* it with her family and all the Theo questions?

Kyros's eyes narrowed. "You don't look like you eat enough over there."

"I'm fine!" She batted away his concerns. She ate plenty. There was no keeping her curves at bay no matter how often she ate like a rabbit. "You must be boiling in that suit."

"This?" He did a twirl in his firefighter's gear. "I suit it well, don't I?"

"Still the show-off, I see."

"Absolutely!" He winked, then just as quickly his expression turned sober. "And now I'd better show off how good I am at helping. There are still a few dozen people unaccounted for. Tourists, mostly."

"Is it as bad as they say on the news?"

He nodded. "Worse. The more we dig, the

more fatalities we find. There are a lot of injuries." He tipped his head down the street. "The clinic was heaving when I was there last. Have you spoken to Theo yet?"

She ignored the question. "How's Leon? I tried to ask Mama a minute ago but the line went—"

She stopped talking as a very large, very exclusive, four-by-four, outside just about any mortal's price range, pulled to a stop beside them. The back window was rolled down centimeter by painstaking centimeter to reveal silver hair, icy cold blue eyes...

Oh, goodness. Theo's father had aged considerably since she'd seen him last. One of the most powerful men on the island seemed to have been unable to hold back the hands of time.

Just about the only thing Dimitri Nikolaides *couldn't* do, Cailey thought bitterly.

"Ah! Miss Tomaras. How...*interesting* to see you back here."

Shards of ice shot through her veins as her brain tumbled back through the years to that day when he'd made it more than clear what he and the rest of his family thought of her.

Nothing but a simple house girl. That's all you'll ever be.

Her brother leaned in over her shoulder.

"Cailey's here to help, Mr. Nikolaides. She's a Class-A nurse now."

"Oh?" A patronizing smile appeared on the old man's face. "You're planning on going to the clinic?"

"To *help*, yes."

She caught her knees just as she was on the brink of genuflecting and stopped herself.

What was she *doing*? Was her body trying to *curtsey*? Good grief! The man wasn't a king and he certainly didn't run the island. Even if he behaved as if he did. And yet there was a part of her that still worried she would never be smart enough, good enough, talented enough to come home and do anything other than fulfil the fate Dimitri Nikolaides had outlined for her.

"I'm sure there's some little corner you'll be able to help out in. Plenty of cuts and scrapes to tend to."

Mr. Nikolaides eyes scanned the length of her, as if assessing a race horse. Working class mule, more like. That was how he viewed her family and it was how he always would.

Cailey's spine stiffened as she forced her static smile not to waver.

"Maternity, wasn't it?"

"S-s-sorry?" *Noooooo! Don't stutter in front of the man.*

"I heard through the grapevine that you help other women with their children. Sweet."

Coming from his mouth, it sounded anything but. Not to mention bordering on pathetic. Women on Mythelios were expected to do nothing less. Cook. Clean. Bow. Scrape. Sometimes she wondered if the island had ever been informed that the twenty-first century had arrived—an era when women were allowed to be smart and have opinions and love whomsoever they chose!

She stared at the lines and wrinkles carved deeply into his face. Saw the cool appraisal of his unclouded eyes. *What made you so mean?*

Once he'd successfully bullied her off the island the man should have had all he wanted. A son to matchmake with the world's most beautiful heiresses. A daughter at an elite medical school. No doubt he knew exactly who *she'd* marry, too. The daughter of his housekeeper was safely out of the picture, so as not to sully his daughter's circle of friends or, more importantly, his son's romantic future.

She forced a polite smile when the silence grew too awkward. "My family usually bundles in wherever help is needed. Leon's police squad is out saving lives this minute."

"*You* don't look too busy," Mr. Nikolaides

glanced at Kyros. "And your mother? Is *she* doing anything or simply enjoying her retirement?"

Cailey almost gasped at his effrontery. Her mother had *earned* her money at the Nikolaides mansion just as she had earned her retirement. And Kyros? Why wasn't *he* saying anything? Why wasn't *she* saying anything?

She'd never let anyone speak to her like this in London. Not after the years of work she'd poured into becoming a nurse. And definitely not after her years of living away from the island to "protect" a billionaire's son. As if Theo needed *protection* from all the European heiresses she'd seen dangling off his arm in the society magazines she might have read accidentally on purpose at the hospital gift shop. On a regular basis.

"Oh, yes. You know us, Mr. Nikolaides," she eventually bit out. "We Tomarases love helping clear up other people's messes."

Mr. Nikolaides blinked. Then smiled. "Yes, we *do* miss your mother's deft touch up at the house. I trust she's well?"

"Couldn't be happier," Cailey snapped.

"Mama's very well, thank you Mr. Nikolaides." Kyros's hand tightened round Cailey's arm. "We're just off now, sir. Glad to see you weren't hurt in the quake."

He turned his sister around and frog-marched her away from the dark-windowed four-by-four, now weaving its way through the rubble strewn along the harborside road as if it had been thrown down by a petulant god.

"What was *that* all about?" Kyros growled.

"Nothing."

He wasn't to know Dimitri had all but packed her bags himself all those years ago. Demanded she never enter the Nikolaides house again. Not as a friend to his daughter Erianthe. Not as a "helping hand" to her mother. And especially not as anything whatsoever to do with Theo, his precious son who was prone to develop "a bleeding heart for the less fortunate."

She launched herself at her brother for a bear hug. It was the easiest way to hide the lie she was about to tell. "I'm just tired after the overnight flight. Once I get to work I'll be fine. It's just weird seeing the island like this."

"I know, huh?"

She could feel his voice rumble in his chest and cinched her arms just a little bit tighter around him. Once she let go of him she'd have to go and face the other Demon of Mythelios.

Full points to Dimitri for pipping her to the

post. But she wouldn't have been surprised if he was stalking the harbor for interlopers. *Huh.*

He looked old. The worn-out kind of old that came from emotional strain rather than physical. Proof he was human? Somewhere in there?

Besides, he'd only put a voice to what Theo and his mates had already been thinking, and no doubt Erianthe too, who hadn't even had the guts to say goodbye to her before winging her way off to her fancy boarding school…

Bah! Enough of putting blame at other people's doors. She'd believed everything Dimitri Nikolaides had said about her because there had been some truth in it. She *wasn't* as smart as the others. She *did* have to work twice as hard to understand things. Finally figuring out she was dyslexic had helped. A bit. But it hadn't made all the medical terminology easier to read. She'd just had to face facts. She wasn't up to Nikolaides standards and no amount of teenage flirtation would change that.

A siren sounded and shouts erupted from a fire truck as it pulled to a stop beside them.

She gave her brother a final squeeze. "Go out there and save some lives." She went up on tiptoe and gave each of Kyros's ruddy cheeks a kiss.

"Same to you, Cailey." He scrubbed a hand through her already wayward hairdo, if you could call stuffing her curls into submission with an elastic band a hairdo. "Welcome back."

She smiled up at him, praying he wouldn't see how their run-in with Dimitri Nikolaides had shaken her to her core. "It's good to be here."

"Is that enough?" Theo was impatient to get back to work. Yes, the media could help. No, he didn't have a moment to spare.

The look on the reporter's face acknowledged the question was rhetorical.

He undid the microphone and began to walk away, ignoring the pleas of the other reporters. They'd be better off showing footage of the rescue crews hard at work while he figured out how to help patients and simultaneously order the urgently needed helicopters to get the worst cases over to Athens.

He could call his dad.

He could also saw off his own hand. Lifting up that phone would come at a cost. It always did.

"Dr. Nikolaides?"

"I'm sorry, I don't have time for any more interviews—"

"No! I'm not with the press. I'm a doctor. My name is Lea Risi."

He stopped and turned. The woman was

wearing holiday clothes. Chinos. A flowery top. Her accent was not local, but she spoke flawless Greek. Useful, considering there was a heavy mix of tourists and locals pouring into the clinic.

For just a nanosecond he rued the appeal of this gorgeous port town that drew holidaymakers from all around the world. If only they were on a rocky outcrop with a diminished population…

"Dr. Nikolaides!" A paramedic was calling him from the hastily put-together triage area off Reception.

He beckoned to Lea. "Come along, then."

"Don't you want to know my credentials?" She ran a few steps to catch up with his long-legged strides.

"Not particularly." He scrubbed a hand through his hair, then pulled the shoulder-length mane back under control with an elastic band he'd picked up somewhere during the course of the day. He didn't know when, exactly. Sixteen hours' straight trauma work did that to a man. The details blurred.

"I'm a psychiatrist."

He nodded. *Fine.* That meant she had medical credentials. "What do you want? Old or young?"

"Sorry?"

"We've got patients coming in from a care home and a school. Both were hit hard. We're triaging on site and transporting to hospital with limited resources."

He stopped and wheeled round, holding out his hands to steady her when she lost her balance trying not to collide with him.

"Apologies." He shook his head. "I'm a bit short on manners today."

"I totally understand. I just want to help."

Theo put out a hand. "Good. Help is what we need. Theo Nikolaides." They shared a quick handshake as he rattled off the necessary facts. "I run the clinic. With the help of some friends. Doctors."

He silently reeled through the cities in the world where they might be. Was Deakin in Paris or Buenos Aires this month? And Christos…? New York. Definitely New York. Ares? Only heaven knew.

Burn specialist.

Neurosurgeon.

Miracle-worker.

If only they were all pilots. He needed them here. But they'd come…they would come.

"Put me wherever you think I'll be best placed—"

Lea was about to say something else when his eyes latched on to a set of unruly curls weaving its way through the crowd jamming up the entryway into the clinic.

Christos!

A jolt of lightning would have affected him less.

What was Cailey Tomaras doing here? The last time he'd seen her—

"Doctor?"

"Sorry. I'm a bit frazzled." He tapped the side of his head. "What did you say your name was again?"

"Leanora Risi. Lea. Just call me Lea."

Her empathetic smile spoke volumes. She could see he was busy, but she wanted to help—and at this juncture he needed all the help he could get.

His eyes slipped past Lea again. Cailey had left the island to become a maternity nurse, hadn't she? Good for her. He knew she'd always been interested in medicine—

"If there's someone else you'd rather I speak with…" Lea put a hand on his arm.

"No. I'm your man. Apologies. There's just someone I—"

Someone I should've kissed ten years ago. Someone I should've taken on a proper date. Someone I never thought I'd see again.

He looked down at Lea's feet and saw strappy

sandals not wholly suited to working in a chaotic clinic.

"Here on holiday?"

"I was." Lea tipped her head and tried to cap-
ture his attention. "But now I'm here to help.
I don't have any equipment but I have these."
She lifted up her hands and twisted them as if
they were freshly washed for surgery.

"Perfect. Good."

Wholly distracted, he let his attention shift
past Lea yet again.

Cailey face had grown…not thinner…just…
Well, even more beautiful, obviously. She'd had
quite a lead in that department. Her cheekbones
had become more elegantly defined…her lips
were still that deep red, difficult to believe it
was real and not painted on…

Had she finally come home?

"Dr. Nikolaides…?" Lea's expression shifted
to one of grim determination. "You obviously
need to be elsewhere. Now, I haven't practiced
emergency medicine in a while. But I'm definitely up to the cuts and bruises variety of
injury—if you'll just point me in the right direction I can get on with helping patients."

"Yes. Of course."

He gave himself a sharp shake. He wasn't
here to ogle ghosts from the past. There were

very real, very urgent medical cases that needed help. *Now.*

"Why don't you go grab a notebook from Petra? She's the loving but steel-hearted battleax working the main desk. She'll give you everything you need to work your way through the queue and categorize people. We've got a couple of doctors working just through that archway. It's makeshift, but we aren't really kitted out for intensive care. I'll be there shortly. There are a couple more volunteer doctors from the mainland seeing less urgent cases."

He looked up to the skylight above them as a medical helicopter flew overhead.

"And a medevac. If we're lucky, we'll soon have one very talented nurse on board as well."

Lea gave his arm a quick squeeze, then headed toward Reception to start work. If she'd said something to him, he wouldn't have known. All he wanted to know was what had brought Cailey back to the island she'd sworn never to set foot on again.

CHAPTER FOUR

"WELL, LOOK WHO we have here. If it isn't Little Miss I'm-Going-to-Make-a-Difference."

Theo Nikolaides. As she lived and breathed… barely.

She opened her mouth. She'd prepared for this. Spent hours of her life thinking about what to say when and if she ever saw him again.

Fffzzzzttt! There went her ability to use actual words.

"Come to help out at our little backwater clinic, have you?"

"I…uh…"

Kaboom! An explosion of fireworks she was clearly powerless to resist went off in her chest, then her belly, then her… Well, everywhere, really.

"Cailey? Are you all right? You haven't been hurt, have you?"

Crrrrassssh! Down came the defenses she'd worked so hard to build up.

She batted away his hand as he reached toward her. She wasn't ready yet. For *that* voice. *Those* words. His *kindness*.

Her cheeks burned at the memory of their heated exchange all those years ago. She forced herself to swallow the array of comebacks she could've spat back, and instead shifted the infant she'd been cuddling back into the arms of his mother.

Prove you've grown up. Prove you've made something of yourself!

"It looks like a superficial wound to me. Cuts always bleed a lot. Just keep the pressure on and I'm sure the good doctor here will get to you as soon as possible."

"Absolutely." Theo gave the mum a quick nod in Lea's direction. "Dr. Risi will be down in a minute to log the case, and we'll get someone to see you and this little one as soon as possible."

Cailey watched, transfixed, as Theo ran his index finger along the infant's face. How could someone so incredibly caring leave his father to do his talking for him?

Pffft. They'd both been young and stupid. At least *she* had been. On too many fronts.

Didn't mean they could kiss and make-up, though.

A vivid image of Theo pulling her roughly

to him for a hot, heated kiss swept through her body. And then she crushed it. That was all in the past.

"How funny—you remember my goal." She turned on her brightest smile. "Mission accomplished. I *am* here to make a difference, thank you very much. A good one. So, if you don't mind putting one of the 'little people' to work, I'll happily get out of your way."

Sea-green eyes bored into her from a face featuring the strong, evenly planed cheekbones she'd dreamt of tracing with first a finger... then her lips...

He was looking at her curiously. She shifted under his gaze, not enjoying the intense scrutiny.

"Here I was, thinking an earthquake would've reminded you that we're all born equal," he said blandly.

It would've been a hell of a *touché* if she hadn't known for a fact he thought she was in an intellectual league well below him.

She held her ground, arched an eyebrow that might have looked defensive but was in fact proud and resilient and completely without insecurity. She hadn't knuckled down for years of painstaking study, work and paying off student loans to get this far only to feel belittled again.

"I think you would probably be most useful

working alongside me. C'mon." He scooped up her backpack, turned and signaled for her to follow him. "Let's get you some scrubs and then you can show me what you're made of."

He put his hand on the small of her back and began steering her through the crowd, using his own body as a shield against the push and surge of people desperate to see a doctor.

While her infuriated brain shot off in one direction Cailey's body was actively registering Theo's on a much more primal level. All six-foot-something, long-legged, trim-waisted, white-coated package of complete and utter male perfection kept brushing up against her as if…as if they had already shared an intimacy beyond that one perfect kiss…

"I think I can get scrubs on my own, ta." She shot him her best I'm-a-big-girl-now look, eyes sparking as they landed on his amused expression.

"No, you can't. You've never been here before."

"Yeah, but—"

"Yeah, but nothing." He grinned down at her. "You can quit the 'city girl' act, Cailey. You're home now. Time to see what my little *kouklamou* of Mythelios is made of."

It certainly wasn't sugar and spice. Not these days, anyway.

Despite her rising fury, something in her softened as she stomped alongside him to get kitted out in scrubs.

Beautiful doll. He'd always called her that back then. Sure, she'd just been his kid sister's friend. Daughter of his family's housekeeper. But even though they'd never put words to it there'd been *something…* Something *magic* between them.

She'd been absolutely sure of it right up until the moment she'd heard him tell his friends that a Nikolaides would never end up with a cleaner.

And that had been that.

Rage at the memory did nothing to stop her insides from fluttering as his hand shifted on the small of her back. How on earth she'd thought she would be immune to him even after all this time was beyond her.

She stole a glance at him as he stepped to the side to avoid a gurney being wheeled through the packed corridor at high speed.

Theo might not be everybody's cup of tea. He had his flaws. A tiny scar by his eye acquired from daredevil antics in one of his father's olive groves. Hair that always looked as if it could do with a cut. Another small scar just below his nose that only seemed to add to the strength of his unbelievably sensual mouth. Sensual, but male.

Everything about him screamed *alpha*. Masculine. It had since they were young—as if he'd been born vividly aware of the world's mysteries and was just biding his time until the rest of the world caught up. Take it or leave it— that was his attitude. Not cavalier. Or haughty. Simply *knowing*. As if he'd made a deal with the universe to do his part and in exchange…

That was the mystery. She'd never seen him take anything. Not one single solitary time. That was the Theo enigma.

He might talk the talk of a rich, privileged so-and-so, but she'd always thought the shadows that crossed those sea-green eyes of his betrayed greater depths. Hidden sorrows he'd rather keep secret. He'd never bare the heart behind that insanely touchable chest of his.

He turned back to her with a smile still playing on his lips. Trust him to be all calm and relaxed amidst a level of mayhem that would have rendered any sane person tearing out their hair.

"There's no need for a tour of the clinic. Shall we just get to work?"

"I think you're going to want to get out of that top first."

"I…uh…" She looked down at the white top she was wearing that had somehow magically acquired a layer of grime and rolled her eyes. *Kyros*. Her brother had been filthy.

Oh, good grief. Where's your spine? Your vocabulary? Use them!

"It's not— I'm here to…"

What is wrong *with you?*

A nurse skidded to a halt beside Theo and put a hand on her chest to stop him. *Lucky minx.*

"Dr. Nikolaides, we've got five patients coming in the next ambulance."

"Five!"

Two pairs of eyes snapped to her.

"There are only two ambulances on the island. We bring in as many people as they can carry," Theo explained.

There was nothing in his voice beyond passing on information. Where was the derision? Why was he taking his time with her? When had he become so…so…extra-perfect?

Her eyes fixed on Theo's lips as he spoke to the nurse. On the tip of his tongue as it touched and retreated from the smooth run of teeth save one crooked one just to the left of center that she'd always liked. Yet another slight imperfection that made him mysteriously even more perfect.

His tongue swept the length of his lower lip before his teeth snagged that lip and pressed down on it while he thought for a moment when the nurse asked where he wanted the patients. It was like being in a slow-motion version of her teenaged fantasies...before the kissing began.

She watched, still mesmerized, as he released his lip and rattled off a list of updates.

A Mrs. Carnosi with a broken arm needed to go to Cubicle Three while her plaster set. A man was in Recovery on the first floor after a heart attack—could someone find his wife down at the harbor? She was helping the baker, he thought. A four-year-old with a head wound could probably do with some crayons to pass the time as the televisions weren't working. All the children, in fact. There were some in a storage locker along with some paper. He was sure of it. Oh, and he'd organized a water delivery so everyone who entered the clinic could be given a two-liter bottle to see them through their waiting time.

Was there *nothing* the man hadn't thought of? All this while also seeing patients? Where was the young man she'd last seen? Arrogant. Elitist. The one who'd turned against her as easily as kicking a door shut. The one who'd compelled her to scrimp and save and study and learn. To leave her homeland pushed by the towering wave of shame that she would never be good enough for a man like him.

She couldn't have been wrong about him after all of this time. *Could* she?

Theo reached back and gave her shoulder a little pat and a squeeze as another doctor took the nurse's spot and asked him to run his eye across some X-rays. A compound fracture. Were they up to performing the surgery the patient would require?

Vividly aware of Theo's fingers on her shoulder, Cailey was barely capable of lucid thought. Her insides were behaving like electricity cables cut loose in a storm. Sparks flying everywhere. Nothing behaving the way it should.

She squeezed her eyes tight against the warm olive color of Theo's skin. His toned physique. The perfect, capable hands touching her.

Just imagining the man holding a child, helping a *yiayia* to cross the street with her shopping or explaining to a daredevil teen that he couldn't go swimming while his arm was still in a plaster made her insides turn into liquid gold.

Which was all very irritating because she was meant to have become *immune* to Theo Nikolaides.

She forced herself to open her eyes and meet the mossy hues of his irises whilst trying her level best to ignore the fact that the man was in possession of the longest, darkest lashes she'd ever seen. He also had more than a five o'clock shadow, but that indicated he'd been working hard and—surprise, surprise—made him look more like a rock star than an unkempt layabout.

No doubt about it. As a grown man Theo Nikolaides was a living, breathing example of a mortal embodying the majesty of the Greek gods of legend. Zeus, Adonis, Apollo… Eros…

"Shall we get you out of these things?"

Theo was looking pointedly at her filthy top, but her thoughts and his tone suggested anything but an innocent need to improve her hygiene.

Was he…*flirting* with her?

This was taking being cool in the eye of a storm to a whole new level.

Just one lazy scan of her dust-covered body and—*poof!*—just like that she felt naked. Each sweep of his eyes drew her awareness to the cotton brushing against her belly, her breasts, the tingling between her legs that was really, *really* inappropriate seeing as she'd vowed to remain immune to the Nikolaides effect. Not to mention the scores of patients waiting.

Seeing him looking at her the way he was… *hungrily*…she felt a brand-new array of fireworks light up her insides and actual electricity crackle between them.

This was all wrong. There was a crisis happening not inches away. People needed help. Patients needed his attention. *Her* attention.

He'd never looked at her like this before. As if she were an oasis and he'd crawled in from the desert desperate for one thing and one thing only.

The sun abruptly lit up the clinic's central glass dome, its rays filtering down to them through a tumble of rooftop wisteria like film lighting. Dappled. Hints of gold and diamonds.

When Theo tilted his face, green eyes still locked with hers, it was all she could do not to reach into her chest and give him her heart. It had always been his. He'd just never wanted it.

Before she could say anything, though, he held out his arm to clear a path for her toward the rear of the clinic.

Of course the crowd parted. Things like that happened for the Theo Nikolaideses of the world. And the Patera and the Xenakis families. Not to mention the Moustakas family. The four families who commanded the bulk of the island's wealth thanks to their business savvy.

Mopaxeni Shipping. The glittering star of the Aegean Seas and beyond. All those businessmen's sons would inherit untold millions—if not billions. So what on earth was Theo doing here in this small town clinic when the world was his oyster?

"Aren't you meant to be—?"

"Right." Theo cut her off, directing her to a green door at the far end of the corridor. "In here."

She turned and tried to take her bag from him.

He shook his finger—*tick-tock, no, you don't*—in front of her lips. "I'm coming with you."

Great. Just what she'd always dreamed of. Death by proximity to the unrequited love of her life.

She pushed open the swinging door to the changing room. Might as well get it over with.

Theo had absolutely no idea where this cavalier Jack-the-lad attitude he was trying on for size had come from.

He was exhausted. Running on adrenaline. He needed food, coffee, and yet... Was this—? Was he trying to *flirt*? Was this what stress did to him? Or was this what all-grown-up Cailey Tomaras did to him?

There'd been that one time as teens, when they'd all been running around the pool, messing about. He'd grabbed her, and she'd slipped on the grass, and they'd fallen in a tangle of limbs on top of one another and there'd been a moment...a kiss...

Makapi!

There were a thousand other things Theo should be doing besides going down memory lane to find hints of a romance that had never been. A restorative fifteen minutes of sleep. Walking the small wards, filled to bursting wards, and diving in where an extra pair of hands were needed. Helping with rescue efforts.

Not staring at a pretty girl from the past.

She looked good. A far cry from the reedy teenaged girl who had seemed to all but live in the shadows of his father's ridiculous mansion. A full cherry-red mouth. Inky black hair. A deliciously curvy figure he could almost *feel*— as if he'd already tugged her close to him for a passionate embrace.

He scrubbed a hand through his long hair, hearing his father's distinctive voice in his head.

"If you're going to slum it as the island medic, the least you can do is maintain the family reputation. I'll not have you gallivanting round the island with a halfwit cleaner's daughter."

His eyes flicked to Cailey's. Dark. Full of passion and empathy. And, if he wasn't wrong, the smallest dose of fear.

His heart cinched. That she should feel that way around him… His father was a cruel man.

Why he couldn't see that kindness, understanding and empathy were far more effective tools for so-called "people management" was beyond him.

Theo had grown immune to Dimitri's tendency to cut a person to the quick, but Cailey…? He'd never subject her to the ego-lashings his *babbo* had dealt out without a second's thought. And for some reason his father had always had it in for the girl. He'd need to keep her close to him. Far easier to keep her out of harm's way then.

"Are you ready to go straight to work?"

Smooth. Nice way to make a woman who's flown overnight to come and lend a hand welcome.

She narrowed her eyes at him. "You're not going to stand there while I change my clothes, are you?"

Cailey's sharp tone brought him back to the present.

He ran his eyes down the length of her. Long legs. Sensually curved hips making a nice dip at the waist. A tug of desire unexpectedly tightened in his groin. *What the hell?* He was supposed to be exhausted, not horny.

"I'll sit with my back turned."

"Yeah." Cailey's hands landed solidly on her hips. "I don't think so. Say what you need to say and then..." She swirled her finger around in an *out-you-go* gesture.

"Fair enough." Despite himself, he grinned. She was setting parameters. The old Cailey would've been too shy to be so feisty. This new Cailey was becoming more appealing by the minute.

Another tug below his belt line broadened his smile. Quite an impact for an unexpected reunion. One of the earthquake's silver linings, he supposed. Maybe she was strong enough now to stand up to his father.

She pursed her lips and tipped her head from side to side in a *when-are-you-going-to-get-going?* move.

Fine. He got the message. "Right. Here's the story. All hell's broken loose. As you probably know, the quake was strong. It hit this side of the island hardest. A lot of old buildings weren't up to the magnitude. It hit in the afternoon—"

"I know. I know all that," interrupted Cailey impatiently. "I saw the news. Late lunch. Quiet time. Lots of people taking naps... Only the Brits mad enough to go out in the sunshine. You should probably know I specialize in pediatrics and maternity nursing, so if it's—"

"You'll be working with me in urgent care," he cut in. He didn't care how bolshie she was.

He was going to look after her, and the easiest place to do that was in his trauma unit.

"I haven't done trauma for over a year."

"But you've done it. And that's where I need you. Case closed," he said firmly before she could protest.

Her shoulders shot up, her mouth opened, but when she saw his stance go rock-solid she dropped the challenge with a flick of a shrug.

"Casualties? Any idea of the scope yet?" she asked.

"Hundreds." Theo shook his head. "I don't know. Several hundred at the very least. The island's got…what?…fifteen or twenty thousand people on it, so it could be more. Patients are presenting with injuries hitting every level of the spectrum, from cuts and bruises to… well…" His mood sobered at the thought of the older gentleman who'd had a fatal heart attack earlier in the day. "Worse than cuts and bruises."

Unexpectedly, Cailey reached out and took his hand. "Are you sure you don't need some rest? You look awful."

"Ha! Thanks. Don't beat around the bush anymore, do you, Cailey?"

She gave him a sad smile. One that said, *I think you might know why.*

The door to the locker room swung open

and with it came the chaos and mayhem of the quake's aftermath.

"Dr. Nikolaides?" The nurse was halfway out through the door already. "There's a helicopter on approach to collect a couple of patients. We need you to sign off on them. And the ambulance is pulling up now."

"Of course."

He brusquely pointed toward a cabinet. "There are spare scrubs in there. All sizes. Report to trauma when you've changed. You're working with me. And that's an order."

CHAPTER FIVE

CAILEY STARED AT the empty space Theo had just occupied.

What on earth…?

Bossy so-and-so.

Hadn't changed a bit. Still lording it about as if he knew everything which—well, in this case he probably did.

You're working with me. And that's an order.

Typical Nikolaides privilege. Just because she was a nurse, and had failed to get into med school, and had taken twice as long as anyone else to get her nursing degree—

Stop! She didn't need to keep raking it all up again. The all too familiar pounding of her heart suddenly leapt into her head, drowning out everything else as she forced herself to take in a deep, steady inhalation and then breathe out again.

You're a nurse, she told herself. *There are patients. This isn't about you. Or Mr. Bossypants.*

She was scared, that was all. The trauma ward wasn't her optimum work zone. But she'd done it before—admittedly getting one teensy-tiny panic attack on her score card. Never mind. She could do it again—minus the panic attack part. There was no way she was leaving this island with her tail between her legs a second time.

A quick wash and she'd get her priorities back in order. She'd returned to Mythelios to help, not to swish around Theo Nikolaides praying he'd notice her. That ship had long since sailed.

When Cailey entered the trauma area it was sheer madness. The number of people had doubled. The volume was higher. The urgency of tone was even more shrill.

A shot of fear jettisoned through her bloodstream and exploded in her heart. This was a far cry from the calm, hushed corridors of the maternity ward she'd left behind in England. There the serene environment helped her stay calm—particularly when she struggled with writing up notes and tackling new medicines and…well…any new words. They all took extra time. Her brain processed things differently.

For the most part she'd beaten her dyslexia into a new, workable form of submission. But this?

This was bedlam. She was going to have to shore up every ounce of courage and nursing know-how she had to avoid falling to bits. It had happened before and she never wanted to go back there again. Especially not in front of—

"All right? Ready to go?"

Theo.

Theo was putting his arm round her shoulders and giving her a squeeze. Everything faded for an instant as she just...*mmm*...inhaled the scent she hadn't realized was all but stitched into her memory banks.

Could he sense her fear? Had he seen the blood drain from her face when she walked into the trauma unit? Spotted the tremor in her hands before she wove them together to stop their shaking?

He squared himself off in front of her, one large, lovely hand on each shoulder. "Just remember: I'm a humble country doctor and you're a big city nurse. You can do this, *koukla mou.* Okay?"

Surprisingly, the term of endearment wrapped around her like a warm blanket. She looked up into his rich green eyes and drew strength from them, felt her breath steadying as he continued.

"I know it seems crazy in here. It is. But this situation is new to all of us and we will each do the best we can. One patient at a time is how we're going to deal with it. All right? One patient at a time."

When their eyes caught she felt her heart smash against her ribcage. The man was looking straight into her soul, seeing her darkest fears and assuring her he would be there to help no matter what. She stared at his chest, half tempted to reach out and touch it, to see if his heart was doing the same.

When their gazes connected again he was all business. He steered her over to a gurney that was being locked into place by a couple of rescue workers.

"Right! Cailey, this is Artemis Pepolo. I've known *this* feisty teen since she was born."

The dark-haired girl nodded a fraction, the rest of her body contracted tightly in pain.

"Artemis has just been rescued after a pretty uncomfortable night under a beam—but you hung in there, didn't you, my love?"

Artemis's breathing was coming in sharp, staccato bursts and her lips were rapidly draining of color. She tried to smile for Theo but cried out in pain. Her arm lay at an odd angle and one touch to the side of her throat revealed a rapid heart-rate.

"Pneumothorax?" Cailey asked in a low voice.

Theo gave an affirmative nod, his gloved hands running along the girl's ribcage as he spoke. "Good. Yes. Traumatic pneumothorax, in this case. The beams of her house shifted when they were getting her out and broke a couple of ribs. No time to get her X-rayed before we relieve the tension. Can you snap on a pair of gloves, get some oxygen into her and clean her up for a quick chest tube?"

Cailey clenched her eyes tight, forcing herself to picture the chart she'd made for herself on how to go through the procedure. Images always worked better for her than words. Miraculously it came to her in a flood of recognition.

And then, as one, they flew through the treatment as if they'd worked together for years.

After snapping on a pair of gloves from a nearby box, Cailey swiftly pulled an oxygen mask round the girl's head and placed it over her mouth, ensuring the tube was releasing a steady flow. She then took a pair of scissors from a supplies trolley, cut open the girl's top, applied monitors, checked her stats and covered her with a protective sheet, leaving a mid-sized square of her ribcage just below her heart exposed. She swabbed it with a hygiene solution as Theo explained the protocol he was going to follow.

"I'm using point-five percent numbing agent to numb the second intercostal space and then a shot of adrenaline-epinephrine before we insert a pigtail catheter, yes?"

"Not a chest tube?" she asked.

The doctor she'd worked under during her stint in the London trauma unit had been old school. *Very* old school. She wouldn't say it had been entirely his fault she'd had her...blip...but he most certainly hadn't helped.

Theo put the tube over a tiny metal rod. "Most hospitals are using the pigtail catheter now. Far less painful for the patient."

She looked for the sneer, listened for the patronizing tone, and heard neither. Just a doctor explaining the steps he was going to take. But better. A doctor saying his patient's comfort was of paramount importance to him.

And then it was back to business. Cailey gave the region around the fourth and fifth intercostal space of the girl's ribcage a final swipe of cleansing solution and then stood back as Theo expertly inserted the needle into the pleural space, his fingertip holding just above the gauge for a second. Their eyes connected as he smiled.

"Ha. Got it. I can feel the air releasing." He turned to his patient and gave her a gentle smile. "Hang in there, love. We're almost there." He attached a syringe to the needle. "I'll just do a quick aspiration to make sure we get all that extra trapped air out."

Once he was satisfied, he expertly went about inserting the thin wire and tube as if he had done it a thousand times. Within seconds the tube was in, the wire was pulled out and Cailey had attached the tube to a chest drainage system.

"Right, Artie. We'll just leave you here to rest up for a bit and then see about moving you somewhere a bit more peaceful where we can check out that arm, all right?"

He pulled off his gloves, smiled at Cailey and tipped his head toward the main trauma area. "Ready for the next one?"

She was impressed. For a man who professed to be a humble country doctor, he knew his stuff.

"Did you study trauma medicine?" She couldn't help but ask the question after pulling the curtains round Artemis and watching Theo give notes to the nurse who, he'd explained, was in charge of moving patients out of the trauma area.

He nodded. "I thought if I was going to be

running this place on my own sometimes I'd better be prepared."

"You're here alone ?"

"Well, not *alone*, alone. There are interns who come in from Athens to have a spell, but they usually get bored with island life eventually and want to get back to the mainland. And the lads come back on and off at certain times of the year in a sort of unofficial rotation; they're just not here at the moment."

She nodded. He must mean Chris, Deakin and Ares—the other Mopaxeni *malakas* he'd set up the clinic with. She wasn't so sure *malakas* was the right word for them anymore. Miracle workers, more like. This place was a far cry from the crumbling old clinic she'd gone to as a girl. And Theo was completely different from the elitist snob she'd been expecting.

"Right." He rubbed his hands together as if preparing for a fantastic adventure. "How are you with broken bones?"

Broken bones. Fractures. Lacerations. Internal bruising. Heart palpations. A massive blood clot… The list went on.

And no matter what he threw at her Cailey stayed bright, attentive and, much to his surprise, willing to learn. There were holes in her knowledge—as to be expected for someone whose specialty wasn't trauma—but she seemed capable of everything short of reading his mind, and even that was sometimes questionable.

Whatever he needed—a particular gauge of needle, a certain type of suture thread, the correct scalpel—she already had it ready before he could ask for it.

As he opened the curtain for their next patient he stopped. *Ah.* Marina Serkos. They'd gone to school together until his father had deemed the local primary unfit for purpose and shipped him off to boarding school.

"Looks like someone's due soon."

This was his one bugbear. The baby checks. He knew he should be happy for others. Share in the joy of a new innocent life being brought into the world. But all he could think each time he saw a pregnant patient was, *Good luck. You'll need it.*

Not exactly a ringing endorsement for "happy families". But happy families hadn't been the remit in the Nikolaides household. Appearances were everything. No one outside the family knew he wasn't his father's success story. Nor did they know he was adopted. And no one—not even his sister—would ever know his silent vow never to bring a child into this world.

Pawns. That was what he and his sister had been. Pawns in a game that hadn't seemed to have any rules.

"Theo?" Cailey had helped Marina up onto the exam table and was wheeling a sonogram machine into place. "Do you want to do the exam?"

Both women were looking at him a bit oddly. If they'd been exchanging information he hadn't a clue.

He scrubbed his hands over his face and forced a smile. "Apologies, Marina. It's been a long day."

"Marina's worried about her baby," Cailey explained in a confident voice.

Ah! Of course. This was her terrain. He nodded for her to continue. It was a relief not to have to *ooh* and *ah* each time a fist curled, or a hiccough came halfway through an exam. In his darker moments he sometimes wondered if the only thing his fellow islanders could think to do during the slow winter months was procreate.

"She's not experienced any blunt trauma, thank goodness, but when the quake struck she was taking a much-needed nap, I presume…"

Both women smiled at Marina's large bump. She was probably near full term by now.

"Are you at seven months, Marina?"

felt like an idiot doing—and was about to apply a huge dollop of gel when she pulled it back.

"Have you eaten or drunk anything in the past few hours?"

Marina shook her head, then stopped herself. "I did drink a lot, because I remember from my last scan they needed me to have a full bladder. It doesn't take much these days!"

"I'm not surprised." Cailey laughed, then put the gel tube above Marina's stomach. "Ready for the cold?"

Marina flinched as it hit her skin and gave a nervous laugh. "This is my third pregnancy. You'd think I would be used to it by now."

"Skin never gets used to a sudden hit of cold," Cailey soothed as she placed the baton on the far right of Marina's stomach and began the scan. "So...let's see what your little one has got up to."

Theo rocked back on his heels and crossed his arms. It was nice to take a backseat for a change, to watch Cailey slip naturally into a role that obviously suited her. He'd never known why she hadn't followed her dream of becoming a doctor and had instead opted for neonatal nursing, but if her complete calm and confidence at this moment exemplified her professionally he'd bet that London hospital would be holding on to her for dear life. Dedicated quality nurses were like rare jewels—something you kept close.

Soon enough, the tell-tale rush of a liquid-sounding heartbeat was accompanied by the whooshed release of air from everyone's lungs.

The women's eyes connected and together they laughed, then returned their attention to the screen. where they could see the curled-up form of a baby sucking its thumb.

Theo picked up Marina's chart, which Petra had somehow magicked out of the mayhem despite the ongoing chaos at the clinic. "Want me to take notes?"

The women turned to him, almost surprised to see him still there.

"Sure. Feels like a luxury to have a doctor take the notes," Cailey said with a smile.

"Consider it payback for all your excellent help today."

Cailey's brows contracted together briefly, as if she were trying to divine something deeper from his words before turning back to the monitor. "The good news is we have a steady, regular heart-rate. One-thirty."

"Isn't that a bit low?"

"Mmm…it's at the lower end of the spectrum, but well within what we would expect. Anything below one hundred or above one-seventy would be of concern." She winked at

Marina. "Your baby is obviously made of stern stuff! Now, I presume you're up to date on all your antenatal scans?"

"Yep. Dr. Nikolaides makes sure of that."

Theo nodded and lifted up the clipboard as a reminder that he was here to take stats. These lapses into chit-chat with mothers always made him nervous. There were the inevitable questions—when are you planning on tying the knot? Starting a family of your own? Bringing a little shining star into the world for your parents to spoil? Conversations he normally actively avoided.

Cailey threw him a *hold-your-horses* look, but gave him the baby's BP in the same steady voice she'd been using with Marina.

She checked the baby's growth, matched the results with the previous figures and pronounced them excellent. She measured the blood flow between the placenta and the baby, and checked the amniotic fluid.

Cailey pointed at the screen, then clamped her fingers over her mouth. Her fingers dropped to her chin and she threw an *uh-oh* look in Theo's direction before asking Marina, "Do you know if it's a boy or a girl?"

Marina nodded her head. Yes, she did. "It's another boy! I'm going to be officially outnumbered when this one is born." A look of panic crossed her face. "If everything's all right?"

"Well, he's moving around just fine, from what I can see. You probably received a big shock yesterday, and perhaps he was sensing your need for stillness. It sounds pretty scary."

"It was," Marina said. "But now that I know my baby's safe I can relax." She smiled at Cailey. "Have you got any of your own?"

Theo's eyes snapped to Cailey. He knew how well *he* responded to that question…

"No," she said simply, taking the baton off Marina's belly and wiping it clean.

Irritation lanced through him as he finished off the notes.

No. That was it? No, *Maybe one day.* No, *Yes, I've left him back in London with my lover.* No, *Perhaps when I meet the right guy...*

What the hell? What did it matter to him if she wanted children or not?

They all started as shouting erupted beyond the curtained cubicle. There were calls for the defibrillator, for more blood.

Theo didn't need to hear more. "Apologies ladies, I'd better get out there."

"All right if I finish up in here?" Cailey asked, clearing the monitor and scanning equipment to one side.

"Yeah. Fine. You wrap things up then I'll see you out there?"

She nodded.

"Good."

Just a few hours in and already he was growing a little too used to having Cailey by his side.

Which was not good. Because whoever came too close into his orbit would also come into his father's orbit…and that *never* went well.

CHAPTER SIX

"AND IT LOOKS like we're back to a normal BP. Heart-rate is steady."

The team around Theo clapped with relief. Their sixty-five-year-old patient, a local schoolteacher, had been helping rescue crews to pull away rubble when a lifetime's worth of deep-fried squid and a love of the honey-soaked sweets brought to him by his students had caught up to him.

Despite her fatigue, Cailey was riding high. She hadn't helped on a cardiac arrest in ages, and this had been a resounding success. Theo had been amazing. A cool, calm and collected doctor in the eye of a pretty crazy storm.

As an orderly wheeled the patient to a recovery room Cailey couldn't help but express her admiration. "That was *amazing*."

Theo smiled down at her, green eyes alight with the satisfaction that came with a high-adrenaline, high-stakes treatment. He'd never looked more attractive to her than he did at that moment.

All of a sudden her knees went weak and everything flew off balance. Theo's arms were around her in an instant, swirling her into the doorway in a fluid move that would have put a tango dancer to shame.

When she opened her eyes all she could see were his lips. And that teensy little scar her tongue itched to reach out and— *Stop it!* She sucked in a shallow breath, horrified to notice that her breasts were pressing against his chest. They obviously had a mind of their own. Little minxes.

Theo didn't move. *OMG.* Did he…did he *like* it? Like *her*?

Her brain went into overdrive. Was she going to have to rearrange a thousand vows never to succumb to the likes of Theo Nikolaides for the very clinical and reasonable sake of finding out just once what it would be like to…? *Oh... Oh, my...* His thighs were pressed against hers. His hips… He was very, very close. She felt the soft exhalation of his breath against her mouth and wanted more than anything to part her lips and taste him.

She risked a glimpse up into his eyes.

What she saw in them conveyed a thousand

messages. Hope. Interest. Desire. A bit of confusion.

Little wonder! She was feeling about as confused as they came. For starters…why was he holding her in this doorway after she'd swooned like an idiot?

"Aftershocks."

"I'm sorry?" Cailey shook her head, only to hear a collective gasp come from the trauma unit as another one hit.

Theo's hold tightened around her, his tall, lean form curling protectively over her, his hands cupping her head against the rigid doorframe as they waited for the tremor to pass.

When it did he stood back and, as if nothing had happened at all, reached out to tuck a few strands of her disobedient hair behind her ear.

"Are you all right, love? Do you need to take a break? We've got relief doctors coming in from the mainland in about…" his eyes traveled to a nearby wall clock "…twenty minutes or so."

Love? Since when did he call her "love"?

He stifled a yawn.

"I think if anyone deserves a break it's probably you," she said, pleased with her stern tone. Then she reached out to give his arm a *you've-worked-hard* squeeze.

Big mistake.

Go away, tingles and butterflies!

"You look tired, Cailey."

"No, *you* look tired."

He rolled his eyes. *No kidding,* the gesture said. *Of course I'm tired, but I'm in charge.*

A strange need to coddle him seized her. He was great at looking after others, but who looked after him?

Good grief. She wasn't letting herself fall for him again, was she? But then perhaps she had never actually got up again after the first time...

"Cailey..."

"Theo?"

He crossed his arms and fixed her with a classic big brother look. "You should get some rest."

She crossed her arms too, beginning to enjoy this back and forth banter. Never mind the fact that being sassy helped her hide the wave after wave of emotion pummeling her mind, her guts, her heart.

Longing. Desire. Heartache. Lust.

She'd thought she'd lain all those things to rest when she'd boarded that plane bound for London all those years ago.

"Tell me, Cailey, who exactly do you think is going to look after the clinic if I leave?"

His expression of triumph spoke volumes. He thought he'd nailed it.

She glanced past his shoulder and smiled as a group of a dozen-plus doctors shouldering medical kits walked through the double doors leading into the trauma area. Fresh-faced. Ready to work.

"They will."

"What?" Theo turned around and registered the change of events.

"So I guess that's settled, then. We'll *both* take a break."

"Where are you staying?"

Theo was as surprised as Cailey when the question popped out.

She glanced at him, and their eyes caught and held tight.

She was always more than your kid sister's friend.

"I haven't really organized things yet. My brothers are crazy busy with the rescue crews." Cailey looked away, a slight flush blooming on her cheeks as she mumbled, "And I don't really think there's room at my mum's now that—"

"What?" Theo took Cailey's shoulders in his hands, forcing her to look at him. "Is Jacosta all right? Is her home intact?"

Cailey shrugged, tears filming her dark eyes. "She says so, but I've not seen the flat myself."

"Flat? I thought you lived in a house?"

"We did, but…" Cailey looked away, a few poorly hidden tears falling from her eyes as she turned.

"But what?" His chest felt restricted against the strain of his lungs. "Has my father not been paying her retirement pension? Do you want me to speak to him?"

Bloody man! The most tight-fisted billionaire he'd ever come across. Not that he knew scores of them, or anything, but he knew enough to know that money made a man more of who he was at heart. Good, greedy, kind, cruel…it didn't matter. Money was an enabler, and if he thought that for one second—

"No, it's not that. When I left for London she sold the house."

She swiped at her eyes, her expression one of pure defiance. There was a story there, but Cailey wasn't pausing for him to ask any questions.

"The place she's in now is diddy. But it's fine. *She's* fine. We're all fine. The Tomaras clan is, as it always has been, perfectly happy. Earthquake aside."

She quirked an eyebrow, adopted a faint smile and looked up at him, unable to hide the shadows of the past shifting across her features like a slow-moving storm.

Clearly not *all* of the Tomaras clan was happy.

"All right, then. If there's no room for you to stay with her, you'll stay with me."

"What? No." She took a step back and held up her hands. "*No.* Completely unnecessary. You've got—"

"Pish-tosh."

He plucked the old-fashioned English expression from his days at medical school in London. Why had their paths never crossed there? She should have called him. Or Erianthe, who was still there.

He swore silently under his breath. He should have kept a closer eye on Cailey. From now on he would. "You're my responsibility."

"Er…and why *is* that, exactly?"

"Because I said so."

Winning answer, Romeo.

Unsurprisingly, Cailey looked unconvinced.

What was he going to say? That he didn't want his father to see her without him there to protect her? It was true. It was also true that he wouldn't be able to live with himself if he thought for one second Cailey's family had been forced to downsize because of anything his father had done.

Somewhere deep inside that sinewy heart of his, he knew his father loved him. Even if he was "just adopted." But he also knew Dimitri's vow to make him pay for not becoming the son he'd wanted when they'd adopted him all those years ago still held strong.

Anyone might think the man would be *proud* that his son had become a doctor. Healing and supporting the very islanders who had helped make his family rich. But, no. He was meant to have followed in his father's wake, taken up the helm at Mopaxeni Shipping and filled the family coffers even further.

"'Because I said so' doesn't really cut it with me, Theo."

He tipped his head back and forth. Fair enough. Cailey was a spirited, passionate woman. No surprise tht she wasn't falling for the dominant male tack.

"You've worked hard, and tomorrow will be more of the same. *Please*. Come to mine and get some rest."

Better.

"I'm not staying."

He barked out a disbelieving laugh. How could he have forgotten how stubborn she was?

"Yes," he ground out in a non-negotiable voice. "You are. My clinic. My rules. You work for me, and if you want to continue to do so you need some rest. I've got a spare room and a perfectly good bed for you to sleep in. As far as I'm concerned you need to be in it. *Now*."

Cailey's cheeks streaked with red. "Yeah, I don't *think* so."

Theo squared himself in front of her. Rolled his shoulders back. Pulled himself up to his full height.

What was he doing? Presenting himself like a prize stallion?

Idiot. She's exhausted. So are you. Act normal.

He cleared his throat and started again. "Get your things. I'm taking you home."

Way to go caveman. Real smooth.

"Theo, really. I'll be fine."

He smiled, caught by surprise at the way she'd said his name. It sounded like a…a verbal caress. Just the chink in her armor he needed.

"I'm afraid it's non-negotiable, Cailey. Bed. Sleep. I can throw some hot chocolate into the mix, but that's where I draw the line."

What was he? Twelve?

Cailey pressed her feet to the ground, obviously gearing herself up to protest, and then, much to his surprise, suddenly wilted.

Raising her hands, she said, "Fine. You win." She turned her surrendering hands into pistols, "But we need to stop by Stavros's *taverna* so

I can see my mother. And after that just a few hours' sleep then I'm back here, just like everyone else."

"Deal."

He put out his hand, and when she placed hers in his to shake on it he stunned them both by raising her palm to his lips and giving it a kiss.

Cailey virtually ran to the changing room to get her backpack. She wouldn't have been surprised if sparks were flying out of the soles of her trainers.

What was going on?

An earthquake wasn't the only thing that had shaken up the island.

Theo was not the man she had decided he would be. In her head—and in truth she had devoted far too much time to this—he had become a mini-Dimitri. No. Worse. A *Monster* Dimitri. A: because he stood about a foot taller. B: because he was a thousand times more commanding when he chose to be. And C: Theo was a million more miles off-limits and a gazillion times more gorgeous than his father.

But other than that…? Exactly the same.

She pushed into the changing room, ran to the sink, stared at the back of her hand for a minute, debating whether or not to kiss it back, then threw handful after handful of cold water on her face willing her brain to try and match Bad Theo with—well…with *Real* Theo.

The real Theo posed a much greater threat to her. The real Theo, in just one day, had teased apart each of the perfect tight stitches she had carefully inserted over the wound in her heart and burst them wide open again.

The man was an infinity of little perfections. Never mind the tug-your-fingers-through-it hair, the ridiculously green eyes, his athletic physique and utterly kissable mouth… He was an incredible doctor. And she found that about as sexy as it came. He was thoughtful. Empathetic. Resourceful. He was a generous colleague. He hadn't once patronized her or tried to catch her out when she'd hesitated over a medicine vial or which scalpel to pick up when he needed one. Not that it had happened much. From their very first patient he'd actually managed to bring out her A-game.

And now she was going to spend the night at his house.

Her powers of resistance were pitiful. She stared at the mirror above the sink and mimicked herself, "'Okay, Theo. Yes, Theo. Whatever you say, Theo.'" Pathetic!

She'd always imagined her return to Mythelios would be more…*triumphant*, in a dignified and grown-up way. She'd wow him with her cool professionalism and make him realize exactly what he'd lost.

Not fall into his arms at the first sign of an aftershock and then agree to curl up in his guest bedroom only not to sleep because he'd be right next door.

She stared at herself again.

Serious face, this time.

Had she tarred Theo with the same brush as his father? Theo had never told her to get lost. Or to steer clear. Okay, so she had heard him laughing with his mates about a Nikolaides never marrying a housemaid once, and that had stung—singed itself into her psyche probably for ever—but it was *Dimitri* who'd told her to stay away from Theo, not Theo himself. And she wasn't a housemaid anymore.

Besides, there was definitely chemistry between them. No denying that. There always had been.

But what if this was just a tease only for him to push her away again? She knew Theo would never marry her, but she had come back sort of triumphant. She was a nurse in an exclusive hospital. She'd done some cracking good work today. Her mother was free of her need for a Nikolaides paycheck so there'd be no more dangling that fear factor over her head. It still shocked her that Dimitri had said he'd fire her mother if Cailey didn't leave his family alone.

A flame lit sharp and bright inside her. She *would* take Theo up on his invitation. The bed. The hot chocolate. She deserved it.

It might not have been his fault her mother had decided to sell the family home to help Cailey with her nursing school fees, but it *was* his fault for being so ruddy nice she couldn't find a reason to say no to staying with him. And if Dimitri found out about this and tried to exact any kind of vengeance the blame would fall solidly on Theo—and then she'd leave the island and never think of either of them again.

"Ready?" Theo strode into the changing room, scooped up her backpack with one hand, slung it on his shoulder and opened his other arm to create a protective arc around her shoulders as he steered them through the crowds to the front door.

Oh, swoon. Wrinkly scrubs suited him. Then again, being naked probably suited him too. Not that she'd imagined that. *Much.*

He pushed open the front door, his arm still round her and whispered, "Out of the frying pan…"

At first she didn't get it—and then just a few footsteps beyond the clinic a whole new raft of sensations bombarded her.

Discordancy. The shrill sounds of heavy machinery hammering away at centuries-old rock and beam. The savaged spot-lit remains of homes and businesses that had virtually disintegrated when the quake had hit.

A wash of guilt rushed over her that she could have been thinking naughty thoughts and having saucy tummy-flips while all this mayhem was still happening across the harbor town.

This was the reason she was here. Not to play out some revenge fantasy against one of the island's richest men.

She shivered beneath the weight of Theo's arm, which was still resting lightly on her shoulders protectively, the way a boyfriend or a husband might touch a loved one who'd had a rough day and was feeling a little fragile.

"You warm enough?"

Theo's voice was soft, a balm against the harsh sound of saws on metal and jackhammers rat-a-tat drumming against concrete.

"Mmm…" She was *confused*, maybe, but not cold. Not with his arm wrapped around her.

Another shiver rattled down her spine at the thought of his father seeing them. He'd warned her off once and this was stark disobedience of the "stay away from my son" remit she'd promised to obey.

But that was years ago.

"Want my jacket?"

"No, no. I'm good."

Scared. Excited. A little bit more lusty than she should be. But strangely...*whole*. As if coming back to the island and finding herself walking side by side with Theo Nikolaides had been the one thing missing from her life.

"Sure?"

He slid his hand to her waist and steered her round some debris that had fallen from a shop front they were passing. The owners sat inside. Their folding chairs flanked an empty crate holding a candle and a half-empty bottle of ouzo. The pair, who must be husband and wife, lifted their glasses when they saw Cailey and Theo passing.

"Yasou!" the pair called out in tandem, then downed their drinks, wincing against the angelica and mace-flavored liquor.

Cheers? Seriously? With their house fallen to bits round them?

"Yasou!" Theo called back, smiling warmly at Cailey, then quickly tightening his fingers at her waist and tugging her out of the path of a couple of smashed watermelons that had been squirted out beneath a collapsed canopy.

"Making the best of a bad lot?" Theo called over his shoulder.

In Greek they called out the age-old saying, "Everything in its time, and in August…mackerel!"

Despite herself, Cailey giggled. "They're certainly optimistic."

Theo shrugged. "They've probably seen worse."

Cailey pulled back, and the warmth of Theo's fingers shifted easily to the small of her back as if they'd been a couple forever. "Worse than their shop crashing to bits when they both look on the brink of retirement?"

Theo stuck out his lower lip and tilted his chin. "First: people like them *never* retire. Second: a bit of patient-doctor privilege sometimes gives an insight into how people prioritize what is bad and what is worth raising a glass for."

Ah. A "big picture" response. She got it. Theo was saying a mashed-up shop was nothing to what that couple had already faced on a personal level. They might have lost a child. Battled cancer. Survived a serious accident. Whatever it was had already put this couple face to face with their mortality—and this time, after the huge quake that had taken over a dozen lives already, they had survived. So why not toast one another?

She glanced back at the couple, merrily refilling their glasses and laughing quietly to one another. Bad things happened, but it was how you responded to them that mattered.

Like deciding whether or not to be frightened of a man who no longer held her family's purse strings. Or of his son who, when you looked at him "big picture" style, was little short of perfect.

CHAPTER SEVEN

"*CAILEY-OULA!*"

Theo retracted his hand from Cailey's waist at the sound of her brother's voice emerging from the rising and falling chatter across the street at Stavros's *taverna*.

It wasn't strange at all for Greeks to show one another physical affection, but it was now that disaster had struck that Theo realized his protective older brother feelings had morphed into *I really want to kiss you* ones.

At the sound of Leon's voice Cailey unleashed the fullest smile he'd seen since her arrival. Bright, full of energy, eyes sparkling as if she *hadn't* just spent the past twelve hours working her heart out.

A swift tug and a tightening right where it counted hit him hard and fast. Oh, yes. His intentions toward her were definitely romantic.

"Kyros! Leon!"

Cailey was up and being hugged in a big

brother sandwich before he'd even had a chance
to get his head round the fact that she wasn't
standing next to him anymore. The crowd was
so thick at Stavros's it would have been no surprise to find half the island's population were
there on the flower-laced veranda. A veranda
miraculously untouched by the quake.

A rapid-fire exchange of information passed
between the siblings in a shorthand he almost
envied. Wives? Great. Where were they? Serving food—just like everyone else. Stavros and
Jacosta had organized it. Where was Mama?
Serving her famous *souvlaki*.

Cailey moaned, kissed the tips of her fingers
and lifted them to the starlit sky. Theo's stomach rumbled. He too had moaned with pleasure
over Jacosta's *souvlaki* on days when his father
had been out of town and he'd "slummed it" in
the kitchen.

Shouts were being launched in the direction
of the *taverna*. "Theo! What are you doing
standing over there by yourself?"

Jacosta appeared next to her children and
beckoned for him to join them, her arms wide
open. As ever she was non-judgmental, wel-
coming, loving.

For the first time in his life he hesitated. How
strange to suddenly feel like an outsider on his
own island. This had never happened before.

Neither had wanting to completely rip the clothes off a woman he'd known since childhood.

The earth wasn't the only thing that had shifted that day.

"Come! Come!"

Jacosta had him in a warm embrace before he had another moment to think. Kisses were exchanged. The standard questions peppered him: "Are you all right? Is your home all right? How is your *mama*? Is her ankle elevated? I heard she twisted it. Your father? I saw him driving past, so I took it as a good sign. Cousins? Aunts? Uncles? Are you hungry? Eat. Eat. Look at you. Skin and bones. You must eat!"

He laughed and succumbed to the hug she pressed him into. It was pointless to resist Jacosta's entreaties for a hug from her "third son."

Wouldn't life have been different if only he'd been adopted by a family for love, not power. He stiffened at the thought and, as if sensing his conflicted feelings, Jacosta let him go.

It was his body protecting his emotions. Protecting them from the inevitable hurt that would come if he so much as *thought* of having a family of his own one day.

"Theo." Jacosta crooked a finger, indicating that she wanted him to come closer. Not that Cailey and her brothers, who were still in the full flow of information exchange, would overhear.

"I hope you are keeping an eye on my daughter." She tapped the side of her nose and smiled gently. "Look after her. She may act the brave one, but she's tender inside."

A huge cheer erupted from the overspill of villagers at Stavros's, followed by an excited gabble of conversation.

Jacosta gave Theo a knowing look. One that said, *I know you know her as well as I do...so be kind.*

Cailey twirled round toward them with a huge smile on her face. "They've found Stavros's cousin's daughter!"

"Wonderful." Jacosta pressed her hands into the prayer position and lifted her eyes to the clear sky up above.

"Mama!" Cailey gave her mother a huge squeeze. "Why are you crying?"

"I'm just so happy. So relieved to have all my children here." She reached out her hands, and a sob of relief filled the air around them as she pulled Cailey closer and then called her boys over for a big, tight family hug.

Something that would never happen in my family, Theo thought darkly. His father had only called to say he'd chartered a helicopter to come to the mansion and fly his mother to the mainland for treatment on her ankle and her nerves, and then asked if Theo was "keeping up appearances" with the clinic.

He couldn't believe his father still didn't get it. That he loved being the island doctor. No, he wasn't a specialist surgeon like his mates—the other "golden boys" of the Mopaxeni founders—but he loved it. Loved helping carpenters and fishermen and cherished ever-aging *yiayias* and even billionaires. Not that his father would deign to receive treatment from *him*. Too personal. Too much like needing the son he claimed was nothing but a disappointment to him.

He scrubbed his hands through his hair. *Enough.* He was tired. Hungry. No point in getting all emotional over a family who liked to hug just because his didn't.

"Come! Theo." Jacosta waved him over to their small group. "Give me a kiss, then go in and make yourself useful. Fetch this poor girl some *souvlaki.*"

She turned to her daughter and they had a swift, low-voiced exchange. He caught the words "sofa" and "extra blankets". Cailey's eyes flicked to his, then guiltily back to her mother's. Jacosta shot him raised eyebrows, clearly went through some mental calculations then offered him an *aha-you-sly-dog* smile.

"I've got food at home, Jacosta," he said.

"What's wrong with the food we have here?" Jacosta's smile shifted to a frown. "You've never turned down my *souvlaki* before."

She lowered her gaze to half-mast and tilted up her chin, her expression wreathed in suspicion. He'd seen this look before. Mostly when his father had exploded about something ridiculous and Cailey had been present. Jacosta had always swiftly shifted Cailey behind her, literally protecting her from the verbal lashing, bowing her head, apologizing, taking every blow he unleashed.

He didn't like being on the receiving end of that look. He wasn't his father. The last thing he wanted to do was hurt Cailey.

"Mama, it's fine. Volunteers have brought food to the clinic. Why don't we eat together later? As a family, when this is over. Then we will have a reason to celebrate, yes?"

"Paidi mou!" Jacosta threw her hands into the air in disbelief. "It's not reason enough to celebrate that my daughter has come home? That her brothers still have life coursing through their veins? That your *mama*'s *souvlaki* is being devoured by all these good people who have escaped with their lives but my own flesh and blood won't take even the tiniest of bites to add some flesh to her body?"

"Yes, of course, Mama, but…" Cailey pressed her thumbs above her eyes and gave her forehead a rub, surreptitiously appealing to Theo for help with a sideways grimace.

Theo swept a hand across his mouth to hide his smile as a glimpse of the teenage Cailey emerged.

"It's been a long day," he said placatingly to Jacosta.

"So she should *eat*!"

"I need to *sleep*, Mama!"

"Mama, let her go." Kyros appeared through the crowd with two takeaway packets wafting the alluring scent of Jacosta's *souvlaki* in their direction. He kissed his mother's cheek, then handed the boxes to Cailey with a wink.

"Now, go!" Kyros made shooing movements with his hands as if he were clearing the area of chickens. "Get some rest, then come back and fix more people. I'm not going to bust my gut rescuing people only to find the clinic staff falling asleep on the job."

His grime-streaked face turned from teasing to sober.

"My wife's nephew is still missing. He went off to play before the quake and they haven't seen him since. There's a crew out there searching right now."

Cailey reached out and gave his arm a squeeze. "I'm so sorry. How old is he?"

"Six."

They all stood for a moment, weighed down by the ramifications. The weather wasn't yet obscenely hot, but spring often saw the temperature gauge fly up unexpectedly, and the longer someone was trapped the more likely it was they'd suffer from severe dehydration. What happened next wasn't worth considering.

"Fine." Jacosta wiped her hands together as if she'd been behind the decision for Theo and Cailey to leave all along. "Off you go. *Shoo*! Get some rest. I'll bring you some yoghurt and fruit in the morning."

Cailey took a deep breath as if to protest, then clearly remembered it would do no good and surrendered to the hug her mother was drawing her into.

Another round of kisses were exchanged and then they were back on their way.

"Your mother is a force of nature."

"That's putting it mildly," Cailey replied dryly, then sucked in a sharp breath as first her spine and then her whole body responded to Theo's touch when he replaced his hand on the small of her back to steer her onto a small tree-lined street that led away from the village's main thoroughfare.

Who *was* this man?

He was much more comfortable with the villagers than she'd anticipated. No lofty heights. No clear social barriers up between him and them.

Had he really changed from that arrogant teen she'd overheard telling his friends about the heiresses his father had lined up for him to marry into this...this kind, generous-hearted, self-effacing man?

There weren't any heiresses in sight now. And—not that she was obsessed or anything— but the pictures of Theo with some willowy blonde on his arm had dried up in the society mags of late.

She chanced a glance at him as he ruffled a child's hair after the little one had run out to show him the bandage he'd applied earlier to her arm. He knelt down and gave it a studied look, then praised her for looking after it so well.

Crikey, that was sweet. *He* was sweet.

Just feeling Theo's broad hand reassert itself on the small of her back relit a flame in her core she now knew had never really been fully tamped out.

As they continued walking she couldn't stop

the niggling thought that ten years ago she'd blown the whole "Nikolaideses don't marry housemaids" thing out of proportion. Had she, a teen herself, taken umbrage for something she should've just laughed off? Or, better yet, should she have flounced out of the pool house she'd been cleaning, flicked a hip in his direction with a saucy follow-up that he didn't know what he was missing?

Instead she'd been upset, hurt and offended. Leaving had been an easy way to protect her heart from feelings she'd thought would never be reciprocated.

Theo slowed his pace and dropped his hand from her back. She missed his touch instantly. How quickly she'd grown used to something she thought she'd never know.

He stopped in front of a large wooden gate and dug his hand round in his pocket, presumably for a key, his shaggy hair falling forward across his darkly stubbled cheeks.

Theo must have felt her gaze on him. He raised his eyes to meet hers and dropped a slow, dark-lashed wink in her direction as he pulled something out of his pocket with a flourish.

"Ta-da!"

She stared at the object in his hand. A mini-screwdriver?

"Man's best friend."

"A screwdriver?" she deadpanned.

"Absolutely." Theo gave her a quick nod, then turned to the gate. "I lost the key about three years ago, and last winter it started jamming, so…"

He fiddled a bit with the screwdriver at an area on the doorframe that looked as if it had borne this routine more than a few times, then gave the door a swift kick. "*Voila!* Your boudoir awaits, *mademoiselle*!"

Trying to push aside images of Theo sweeping her off her feet and carrying her to said boudoir, she tried to wrangle her backpack off his shoulder.

"No, you don't." Theo swept his arm out, indicating that she should enter the small but incredibly lush garden where a smattering of golden sandstone slates led to a modest-sized whitewashed traditional home. "In you go." He pulled the gate shut behind them as she entered the garden. "So. What do you think?"

What did she *think*? She thought it was the last sort of place a Nikolaides would live in. More to the point, she thought it was perfect.

The small house was precisely the type of a home she'd dreamt of living in before she'd left the island. Draped in bougainvillea, shaded by palms and…was that a pomegranate tree? It felt…cozy. It was about as far as you could get from the ostentatious steel beams, floor-to-ceiling glass and columns of the neo-classical mansion he'd grown up in.

There went a few more of her hypothetical conjectures about The Life of Theo.

"I think it's beautiful."

He squinted at her, the corners of his lips tweaking up into a quirky smile. "Excellent. And it looks like the chaps who did the stone-masonry all those years ago knew what they were doing."

"What?"

"No cracks from the earthquake."

"Haven't you been—?" She stopped herself. Of *course* he hadn't been home yet. He'd been at the clinic yesterday afternoon when the quake struck and hadn't been home since.

In lieu of throwing herself at him and telling him how selfless and wonderful he was, she shifted her weight on her heels and gave the house a studied look.

"How old is it, exactly?"

"Hmm…" Theo drummed his fingers on his chin and stared at the house as if someone would pop out of the front door and tell him.

My goodness, he has a lovely jawline. Had she ever even noticed a man's jawline before?

"Not very. Three hundred years old? Maybe four? Not dawn of civilization stuff."

Cailey couldn't help but laugh. She'd always held a deep affection for the neglected and often abandoned stone structures dotted about the island. How funny that Theo seemed to share the exact same level of enthusiasm. He took a few long-legged steps past her and opened the thick wooden door to the house.

"You have the key to this one?" she teased, feeling a strange new store of energy coming to the fore.

"Never locked." He looked back at her and gave her another one of those butterfly-inducing winks. "Wait here for a minute while I check the structure. It would be a bit embarrassing if your bedroom had been swept out to sea."

Double swoon!

There was no doubt about it. Theo was flirting with her and she was falling for it hook, line and sinker. Just as she'd warned herself not to.

Then again… If this whole "get some rest at my house" thing was leading where she thought it might, it could lay a few old demons to rest.

Yes. Definitely. They'd have their night of carnal bliss and then *poof!* She'd lend a hand for a few more days at the clinic, maybe throw in a bit of a showdown with Dimitri, then get back to her job in London, put an end to the evil glares of the gift shop lady every time she leafed through the society mags, and get on with the rest of her life.

And maybe monkeys wearing tiaras would fly out of her backpack.

Theo appeared at the doorway. "It's safe. Still no power so I've lit some candles. Just a couple of broken plates." He laughed. "Typical Greek, eh? Breaking plates in the best and worst of times. C'mon. In you come."

He crooked his finger, beckoning to her like the wicked wolf luring little Red Riding Hood into his lair.

Goosebumps skimmed across her skin as she stepped inside. Like the outside, the interior had the gentle glow of whitewashed stone walls. Theo had lit several candles set in traditional wall stands complete with mirrors, so a soft, warm light flickered around the room.

The ceilings were higher than she'd expected. The odd exposed support beam added character. Wooden, of course. A small kitchen was tucked at the back of the large open-plan area, so that there was room for a circular dining table opposite a pair of French windows. In the living room area, where they stood, a pair of over-sized sofas, perfect for napping or reading on, were dotted with blue throw pillows. The sofas faced another set of French windows, leading to a covered veranda, beyond which she could just see the white effervescent foam of the sea—still a bit choppy, though there had been no aftershocks since the one a few hours ago.

"It's beautiful."

"Not as beautiful as you've become, Cailey."

Theo was right behind her, his voice low and weighted with intention.

She wheeled round and stumbled back a few steps. Being so close, inhaling his scent—amazingly pure and clean after such a long day—was suddenly too much.

"Why are you being so nice to me?"

Theo actually looked shocked at her question. "Why shouldn't I be?"

Cailey was about to launch into a rather detailed explanation of exactly *why* this was all rather peculiar when he closed the space between them and put a finger to her lips.

"Cailey *mou*. I've always felt we had a connection, you and I. Don't you know that?"

She shook her head against his finger, fighting the urge to open her lips and draw it into her mouth. Any connection they'd had had been more master and servant than anything. She'd grown up working in his house. Scrubbing, cooking and cleaning alongside her mother, who had spent her entire adult life serving as the Nikolaides housekeeper.

Sure, she'd played with Erianthe when they were kids, and sometimes with Theo when he and his gang were in the mood to torture or tolerate his kid sister, but a *connection*…? She'd thought that kiss they'd shared all those years ago had been a dare. A cruel one at that. For it had been only a day later when she'd overheard him telling his friends he'd never marry a housemaid.

She was surprised to see him looking hurt. Genuinely hurt. Furrowed brow. Eyes narrowing. A sharp intake of breath. The whole caboodle.

"Not in the strictest sense," she whispered against his finger.

"We're peas in a pod. You must know that. And today, working together, wasn't that proof?"

"No. It only proves we work well together. Our lives…we're so different."

She wanted to hear him say it. Say he'd held himself apart from her because of her background. That he'd soared where she had failed even to get into medical school, let alone become a doctor.

"You *are* different from me," he said, lowering his head until his lips whispered against hers. "You're better."

Before she could craft a single lucid thought

they were kissing. Softly at first. Not tentatively, as a pair of teenagers might have approached their first kiss, more as if each touch, each moment they were sharing, spoke to the fact that they had belonged together all along.

Simply kissing him was an erotic pleasure on its own. The short walk to Theo's house had given his lips a slight tang of the sea. Emboldened by his sure touch, Cailey swept her tongue along Theo's lower lip, a trill of excitement following in the wake of his moan of approbation.

The kisses grew in strength and depth. Theo pulled her closer to him, his lips parting to taste and explore her mouth. The hunger and fatigue they'd felt on leaving the clinic were swept into the dark shadows as light and energy grew within each of them like a living force of its own.

Undiluted sexual attraction flared hot and bright within her, the flames licking at her belly, her breasts, her inner thighs, as if it had been waiting for exactly this moment to present itself. Molten, age-old, pent-up, magically realized and released desire.

CHAPTER EIGHT

"Come, *koukla mou*."

Theo pulled one of the candles off its stand and took Cailey by the hand. He led her to a doorway on the far side of the living room, barely knowing where his energy was coming from. A stress release after such an intense day? A primal need to remind himself of his mortal ability to weather such an extreme act of nature?

Or was it something much more simple? Like fate?

He turned to her and released the riot of curls from the wooden hairclip barely managing to hold her inky black hair in place. She flushed and looked to the floor as silky waves cascaded around her shoulders.

"Are you sure this is what you want?" His voice sounded hoarse. A sure sign that his emotions had taken over.

She turned her head and gave looked at him askance. It was a look that said, *Are you?*

"*Thee mou…* I've thought about you—about this—all day. I just want you to be sure. If this is your first time—"

She cut him off with a shake of her head. "This isn't my first time. But…"

He swept his fingers along her face. "But what? You can talk to me, Cailey."

She looked him straight in the eye and said, "You're the first man I ever wanted."

Her words roiled through him like molten lava.

"Come here, you."

He tugged her to him, blood pounding through his veins, powering the need to taste, touch, taunt…and fulfil her every desire.

Cailey tutted playfully. "I've waited twenty-seven years for this…let's take it slow."

She pushed his hands down, then began with trembling fingers to unbutton his shirt.

He lifted her hands to his lips and kissed each of her fingertips. "Don't be scared. It's only me."

Her cheeks pinkened. "That's precisely why I'm shaking, you fool."

"I don't frighten you, do I?" He almost laughed at the absurdity of it.

"No." She shook her head. "It's how I *feel* about you that frightens me."

She looked so vulnerable the only thing he

could do was pull her to him and whisper into her ear that she could trust him. He meant it, too. And couldn't imagine making the promise to anyone else.

"How do I know?"

He held her away, so he could look her straight in the eye as he said, "Because I feel exactly the same way as you do."

"What? Excited, terrified and itching to get naked all at once?"

He laughed softly. "That about captures it."

She tipped her head to the side, as if ascertaining whether he meant it. "You're not quite who I thought you were, Theo Nikolaides."

"Oh? And who exactly *did* you think I was?"

She shook her head, "I'm not really sure anymore, but…" She lowered her lashes then opened her eyes with a teasing flash of a smile. "Do you think we should just go for it?"

"I think that's a most excellent idea." He laughed again, before weaving his fingers through hers. "Come on." He led her to the big sprawling bed he'd indulged himself with when he'd bought the place. "Let's spend as long as we need to get to know one another all over again."

She held her ground. "Sorry. Just one more little thing. Can we have a no-strings-attached rule? Like, what goes on at the earthquake… stays at the earthquake?"

"If you wish." He shot her a sidelong look. "Unless it's to keep this a secret from a boy-friend back in London?"

"No." She sucked in a quick breath. "No boy-friend. Just big brothers…and a mother who seems to find out everything anyhow and… well…your father."

"My father?" He barely recognized his own voice it had hollowed out so quickly. "What's *he* got to do with anything?"

"I don't really think he likes me."

"Well, I don't like *him* very much." The bas-tard. If he'd so much as said a single word to her…

Cailey's eyes widened. "Really?"

"Really."

He flicked a switch in his head. He didn't want to be talking about his father right now. Or anyone else, for that matter.

"C'mere, you." He pulled her over to the bed and straddled her before pressing his lips gen-tly to hers. "What goes on at the earthquake… stays at the earthquake."

He took Cailey's hands and put them back on his chest as he dipped his lips to hers for another deep, erotically charged kiss. Feeling her breasts press up into his chest, her nipples taut with anticipation, sent a surge of blazing heat straight to his groin.

He gave the hem of her scrubs top a gentle tug. "May I?"

She nodded, her eyes sparkling in the candlelight.

He slowly lifted her top up and off her, his fingers lightly grazing the bands of lace cupping her breasts as he did so. By God she was beautiful. Olive skin. Full breasts. Dark nipples, taut and tempting.

He put the top on a chair by the bed and knelt in front of her. Unable to resist, he softly cupped her breasts, relishing the sensation of lace and warm skin as Cailey wove her fingers through his hair and tugged his head back for an urgent kiss.

Enough with the niceties, her kiss told him. *It's time to get down to business.*

All he could absorb in his overwrought brain was that he wanted more. To touch. Caress. Give her every ounce of pleasure he could.

He curved an arm around her waist and pulled her to him, his fingers cupping one of her breasts as he licked the other one through the gossamer lace barely containing it. He shifted the fabric to one side and gave her nipple a hot, wet lick. Her fingers dug into his hair again, giving him all the permission he needed to continue. Swirling, tasting, touching, caressing...

He forced himself to adopt a more luxurious pace, relishing the soft shudders of approbation as Cailey's body reeled and recovered from the erotic journey of his tongue and lips across her breasts, down to her belly. Shifting across her hips. Making the most of the luscious dips and curves along the way before lowering his lips to her waistline.

His fingers worked slowly, tauntingly, at the butterfly bow she'd tied in her scrub bottoms. Before releasing it, he encouraged her to lie back as he teased two of his fingers over the gently rounded surface of her belly, stopping only to draw in a deep breath of her skin. Vanilla? Or was it honey? The sweet and pure scent of olive oil? Enchantingly indescribable aromas all designed to drive a man wild. Drive *him* wild.

Centimeter by centimeter he lowered her scrubs...then her panties...adoring the shivers of excitement buzzing across her skin as he dropped kisses, little nips and licks, along the swoop from hip to hip and lower until she wove her fingers into his hair and cried out to be with him.

"Not yet. Not yet, *koukla mou*." He spoke the words and his lips whispered against the delicate skin just above the thin strip of hair leading to the soft folds between her legs. "If you have waited this long, I want to make it worth it."

He thought he heard her say, "It already is!" and "Now!" but then her words melted into moans as he slipped his fingers between her legs and stroked the honeyed response to his caresses.

He was as fully erect as he had ever been, and sustaining this level of control was going to be a challenge, but she was worth it. Especially if it was true that she had wanted him all along…

Cailey felt drugged with pleasure as Theo slid his warm, assured hands between her legs and parted them.

She'd had sex before, but she was certain she had never been made love to. And they hadn't done anything much beyond kissing yet!

All the blood in her body surged and collected at the pulsing triangle between her legs as Theo cupped her buttocks in his hands and began to lick her. The level of pleasure he elicited was electrifying. She felt so sensual, so alluring—it was as if he was drawing an inner goddess out of her she'd never known existed. Each of his touches inflamed a deep-seeded pulse from her very essence that grew and hummed until she dug her nails into Theo's shoulders, pressed closer to his lapping tongue and cried out to him to let her release. She tried and failed to stem a wail of sheer ecstasy as her body tightened and arced as wave after wave of pleasure luxuriously swept throughout her body.

Theo held her tight to him after climbing up onto the bed alongside her. "Feeling better?"

"I was never feeling bad," she managed to murmur as she pressed herself to him, seized by the spirit of a tigress.

She'd forgotten he was still wearing clothes. Nerves completely eradicated, she swiftly undid his shirt buttons, then just as quickly unhooked and, in one extraordinary move, whipped off his belt. To their mutual astonishment she gave the length of leather a sharp crack before flinging it to the far side of the simply furnished room.

"My goodness, little one…" Theo said approvingly. "You're full of energy tonight."

Cailey moved her hands to his thick erection. "I'm hardly little, and it's not exactly as if you're running on empty. Shall we see what we can do for *you* now?" She gave the length of his shaft a playful lick.

Where did that come from?

She didn't do sexy talk. Or crack leather belts like a dominatrix. Or demand sex, for that matter.

Being with Theo was dangerous. On far too many levels. But at this exact moment she had no inhibitions—and no ability to stop herself from wanting more. She pushed him back on the bed and crawled on top of him, straddling him with a provocative twitch of her lips.

"Tell me, Doctor. Would you like to have your own turn?"

For a nanosecond he looked confused. When her hand began to stroke the velvet-soft length of his shaft the dawn of realization came quickly. He grinned, clearly amused at the she-woman he'd unleashed, and raised his hands in a move that said, *Do what you will. I'm yours for the taking.*

Cailey pressed herself up onto her hands and knees and swept her breasts along the smooth surface of Theo's well-defined chest. Not weight-lifter bulky...just strong and perfect. She gave each of his dark aureoles a lick and a quick suck before slowly working her way south.

When she first touched his erection with the tip of her tongue he inhaled sharply. When she took him in her mouth he cried out her name, fingers reaching out to touch her hair before falling helplessly to his sides as she had her wanton, wicked way with him. As his pleasure increased, so too did Cailey's. The two-way exchange of pleasure wasn't something she'd considered in all these years of wondering… Yes, she'd had sex before, but this felt different. Powerful. Captivating. Like an awakening.

A heated thrill thrummed to life in the very kernel of her femininity. Giving Theo pleasure was as erotic as receiving it. The more he responded to her touch, the more energized she became. The more she gave, the more he craved.

Abruptly Theo pressed himself up and pulled her alongside him. "I want you, Cailey. *Now.*"

His voice was urgent, full of longing. It was the most uninhibited she had ever seen him. Being the reason for it sent fresh ribbons of pleasure through her. In the clinic Theo was the picture of a man in control. Here, beneath her fingertips, he was vulnerable to her lightest touch. Power and protectiveness wove together as one as she kissed his neck, his throat, his lips.

"I want you," he said again as their mouths parted after another all-encompassing kiss.

There wasn't a single cell in her body capable of saying no. She'd imagined this moment for years…and the reality was light years better than any fantasy she had conjured.

"I'm all yours," she said, meaning each of the words with a totality that came from realizing she'd loved him all along. If this was her one chance to love and be loved she was going to take it. Even if it meant returning to London on her own, she'd have this moment locked in her heart as proof that for one night she had been everything he wanted.

Theo slipped an arm across her belly, then gently shifted her onto her back. "You're sure?" His green eyes were almost black in the flickering half-light the candle afforded them.

She'd barely finished saying yes before she felt the tip of his shaft tease at the heated entrance to her womanhood. She parted her legs in response. Never before had she been so aroused.

Theo moved slowly at first. Teasing the tip of his erection in and out of her until she was nearly mad with euphoria and longing. And then he began to press into her more deeply, each penetration bringing with it another layer of fulfilling pleasure. It wasn't until she begged him that each measured stroke became lost in a shared desire to meet one another thrust for thrust. Restraint was abandoned. Her hips became fine-tuned to his untethered thrusts. Her hands wove tight round his neck, then shifted to his back as she wrapped her legs round him, wanting him to bury himself as deep within her as their longing would permit.

Their shared desire lifted them outside of human constraints and into a timeless eternity. When the rhythm of their lovemaking reached a mutual crescendo, as one they gave themselves to the all-consuming joy of a shared climax before collapsing in a weighted tangle of limbs and desire.

As their breathing began to steady Theo rolled off her, pulling her with him so that they were still joined together.

"My goodness, little one…" He dropped kisses on each of her cheeks and her forehead, "Welcome home."

Cailey gave him a deep kiss in return, then began to giggle as she slipped away from him so they could snuggle under the covers. "I have to admit this is not *quite* the homecoming I was expecting."

"You and me both," Theo teased, wrapping an arm around her shoulders and pulling her close to him so she was nestled against the warm, solid length of his body. "Little Cailey Tomaras is all grown up." He swept a hand along her curves as if to prove it.

"Worth the wait?" she asked.

"And then some."

They lay for a moment in silence, their breathing leveling out, shifting into a cadence matching the susurration of the waves just beyond the bedroom windows.

"That's never happened to me before," Cailey said eventually.

"What? Getting hit on in the midst of a humanitarian crisis?"

"Well, that too." She giggled, still a bit shell-shocked at the dichotomy of the day. And how natural it all seemed.

Work hard. Love hard. *If* that was what this was. It was so easy to be with him. Intuitive, almost.

"I mean the…you know…" Shyness washed over her despite the raw intimacy they'd just shared. "The butterfly magic." She pulled her arm out from under the sheet and pointed to below her waist, whispering, *"Down there."*

Now it was Theo's turn to laugh. He pulled her closer to him and pressed a soft kiss on her forehead. "Is that what the cool kids are calling an orgasm these days?"

"Well, no. But for me it was…"

"Virgin territory?" he countered, a slightly incredulous tone in his playful voice.

"In a manner of speaking."

She looked away, slightly horrified that she'd

brought it up at all. He was obviously experienced and she was a virtual neophyte. One boyfriend. A few rounds of terrible sex. She'd ended the relationship once she'd convinced herself that being alone was better than pretending she was loving it. Loving *him*.

In truth, no one had ever really stood a chance of winning her heart when—love him or hate him—it had always belonged to the tall, olive-skinned, unconventionally handsome doctor now lying naked as a statue of Adonis right next to her, lazily tracing his index finger along her collarbone.

"It's true." She decided to own her history. "This is the first time I've truly experienced pleasure during sex."

Theo propped himself up on his elbow, his mouth curving into a warm smile. "In which case, *koukla mou...* I am both honored and humbled to have brought you that pleasure."

She pressed a soft kiss on his lips, grateful he hadn't crowed about his prowess. But that wasn't the Theo she'd always been attracted to. *He* was truly a kind-hearted, generous man.

Raw emotion scratched at the back of her throat as she took on board the impermanence of what they had just shared. Sheer happenstance had brought them together today. Day-to-day life would surely push them apart. Not to mention his family.

Not wanting him to see her mood shift, she turned around so that they were spooning. Beyond the windows the stars sparkled brightly above the sea. She'd forgotten how clear the sky was here...how nourishing the sound of the waves could be.

She'd always dreamt of living close to the sea. On her mother's salary they'd never been able to afford it. At least her mum could see the Aegean now, from the small balcony of her flat.

Silver linings were everywhere, she reminded herself as Theo's arms tightened around her and eventually they drifted off to sleep as one.

CHAPTER NINE

CAILEY WOKE WARM and nestled in Theo's arms. The early dawn light that was so particular to the island was just reaching its tendrils through the windows, hinting at a sunny day ahead and then, a few moments later, promising one.

She shifted gently in his arms, relishing his scent, the feel of his skin, his…

Oh, no.

Oh, no, no, no, no, *no.*

Her eyes popped wide open as she realized what they had done last night. And more to the point what they hadn't.

Protection!

Years of medical training should have drilled into each of their heads that if they didn't want a baby they should use a condom.

Her skin turned clammy as instant panic took hold. She trawled her mental calendar to remember when she'd had her last period, where she was in her cycle. Her skin went prickly as she counted out the days to her peak fertility zone.

Out the blue she remembered a joke she'd heard someone tell in the maternity ward, when one of the nurses had asked another what you'd call couples who practiced the rhythm method.

The answer?

Gulp.

Parents.

Her mouth went dry as the Sahara as she slid herself as fluidly as she could out of Theo's embrace. She grabbed a pair of fresh scrubs from her backpack and tiptoed to the bathroom. Mercifully the earthquake hadn't affected the island's water supply.

Another aftershock might easily change that small mercy. Could another aftershock send her back in time and help her make better decisions?

She glanced back at Theo, all peaceful and perfect-looking.

Oh, no, no, no, no, no. This was very, *very* bad.

Work.

If she took a shower, downed a coffee…or seven…snuck past Theo and went to work she could get her head screwed on straight and think about what she should do in between the inevitable flow of sutures, bandage applications

and blood pressure tests she'd be performing…
alongside Theo…her boss.

"Hey, there, beautiful."

Cailey yelped in surprise and whirled around,
hoping her mad morning hair and wild-eyed
look would send him running for the hills. That
way she could sort out this mess on her own
and never have to admit she'd been—*they'd*
been—so idiotic. Why she felt the need to protect him from any fallout was a bit strange, but
then *life* was being strange at the moment.

"You're looking ready to take on the day."

Theo's morning grin was slow and lazy.
Dreamy, actually. If her stomach hadn't been
full of a squad of high-octane piranhas it would
have enjoyed the gentle swoop and swirl of butterflies.

How on earth was she going to tell him that
they might have just made the most permanent,
life-changing, baby-shaped oopsie?

"Want me to jump in the shower with you
before we head back to Chaos Central? A little
delicious morning escape before the storm?"

Um… Of course.

But it wasn't as if a bit of soap and water
would help her forget the work that awaited
them. Or the baby they might have made last
night.

The brain knocking around in her skull was

Chaos Central. Not to mention the heart pounding against her ribcage. The arterial pulse popping along the side of her throat.

Couldn't he see it? Didn't she look tachycardic or anything? Ashen? A bit breathless? Or was that the same thing as looking totally in lust for a guy she'd just gone Aphrodite over the night before?

He wove his fingers through her tangle of hair and gave her a soft kiss on the lips. "Mmm…morning breath."

"Theo, sorry, I just—"

"It's all right, *kouklamou*." He swept a finger under her chin and then popped it on the tip of her nose. "Good to know your only need is for a toothbrush and some toothpaste. That much I can do."

He turned to the bathroom, then threw her a grin and a wink.

"It's an airplane amenities bag, FYI. Not a Lothario's stash. Trust me—last night broke a long drought. But it was worth the wait," he quickly added with another kiss. "Absolutely worth it."

"Good. That's great. I mean, I have my own toothbrush in my bag. It's just that—" Cailey tipped her head into her hands and drew a deep breath.

Just say it. Just say it, you idiot.

"You want a coffee?"

Theo's brow was furrowed. He was clearly not quite understanding why his invitation for a shower *à deux* should cause such consternation.

"No!" She squeaked, about an octave higher-pitched than she'd intended, and then she all but shouted, "I need the morning-after pill!"

A loud, insane buzzing took over in her brain. That wasn't strictly what she'd planned to say, or entirely what she'd *wanted* to say—but, hey…maybe Theo had always hoped and dreamed of a shotgun wedding with a bride whose stomach was the size of a watermelon. Not that she even knew if she was pregnant yet…

"Ohh-kaay…"

Theo clearly thought he was humoring a crazy woman—and then she saw him go through his own version of revisiting the night. His brow furrowed again. Eyes drifted up to the right. Fingers drummed along his chin.

It was easy enough to see the wheels turning behind those beautiful green eyes of his. Narrowing at first, then widening. *Not good.* A flash of something dark and dangerous swept across the bright spheres, leaving them a shade darker than forest-green in its wake. A flash that read: *This wasn't meant to happen.* Rapidly followed by, *This is definitely not going to happen.* Not on his watch.

What a fool she'd been. To let herself get swept away like Cinderella at the ball only to realize princes didn't go for girls who rode to parties in pumpkin carriages.

A coolness overtook Theo's entire demeanor and it chilled her to the bone. *This* was the Theo she'd been expecting to see after all these years. The one she'd deluded herself into thinking had been a figment of her imagination.

"Right. Fine. That's what you want to do? Not a problem."

His voice was clipped. All business.

If there was a way to feel invisible and yet like the elephant in the room all at once, Cailey was certainly experiencing it right now.

"Well, it's not exactly what I *want* to do," she snapped. It wasn't like she'd made love to *herself* or anything. "It's just the first thing I thought of."

"Aren't you *on* anything?"

She shook her head. "Like I said, jumping into other people's beds isn't really my *modus operandi*."

"What? You think it's mine?"

She shrugged. "Maybe. What do I know?"

Her insecurities leapt to the fore and against

her better judgment her entire body became a hot shield of defensiveness.

"Lately you haven't been the regular player on the society pages you once were. Forced to slum it with the local talent these days, Theo? Is *that* what's got you so het-up? That you went low-rent?"

Theo started to say something, then stopped himself. "Fighting about this isn't going to fix anything," he said instead.

Everything in her crumbled. He hadn't denied it. Hadn't said anything to convince her she wasn't just common riff-raff to him.

It took all her power to maintain eye contact. "So, what do you suggest we do?"

"Are you sure you're all right with taking the morning-after pill?"

His tone spoke volumes. He wasn't asking the question because he thought it was a bad idea.

She nodded, still clutching her clothes to her naked body. About as exposed and vulnerable as it got. It certainly wasn't the way she'd wanted to have this conversation. Not that she'd wanted to have this conversation in the first place!

She didn't really know if she wanted to take the pill. But she *did* know she was absolutely not going to corner Theo into anything he didn't want. It wasn't as if he was jumping up and down for joy, plucking names out of the ether for their unborn child.

"Absolutely. Not a problem." She kept nodding, as if her neck had turned into a spring. "I'll just jump in the shower, shall I? Then get down to the clinic."

"You'll need me to prescribe it for you."

His voice sounded like cold steel. And there was no meeting her gaze. His eyes looked past her intently, as if she were no longer the woman he'd murmured sweet nothings to all night.

Ha! Those sweet nothings were exactly that. Intangible bits of fluff as useful as a dust mote.

She fought the sting of tears at the back of her throat, silently waiting for the follow-up. The accusation that although she clearly thought she'd risen a rank after her time in London, back here on Mythelios a Nikolaides was still in one league and a Tomaras was decidedly lower.

When none came she slunk off to the shower and scrubbed herself to within an inch of her life, wrestling with an internal tennis match of recriminations.

Why had she come here in the first place? Why hadn't she just stayed with her mum? The sofa wasn't that bad. Besides, her family were the ones who had always been there for her. Helped her find ways to fight her dyslexia. Found the fees for nursing school. English lessons. Private tutors. And yet here she was, years later, still following Theo round like a lovelorn duckling, kidding herself that she was doing it to help her family.

A curl of disgust at her own behavior snapped against her conscience, leaving a vivid mark. She'd done it again. Let her feelings for Theo override her pride. Her dignity.

After her shower she toweled off quickly and pulled on scrubs and trainers, desperate to run to the clinic and get to work—help out as much as she could until the crisis had abated and then hightail it straight back to London, where life as a celibate was looking pretty fine to her right about now.

When she opened the blue wooden bathroom door Theo was leaning against the wall, a towel wrapped round his waist, a steaming cup of coffee in his hand. Thick and dark—the way real Greeks liked it. Her mouth watered. And it wasn't for the coffee. Was this just an additional splash of torture? Showing her what she couldn't have anymore?

He looked up, his expression a mix of contrition and agitation. *Damn*, he was beautiful.

"I was a bit of an ass." He handed her the coffee.

"I didn't want to be the one to say it," she

managed, in as light a voice as she could conjure. The last thing she'd been expecting was an apology. If that was what this was.

She accepted the cup and took a grateful gulp of the inky black coffee. Mmm, she'd missed this. She'd missed *him*.

"I should've sorted out protection last night. Things just got…"

"A bit weird?"

"A bit *wild*," he corrected, the corners of his mouth twitching against a smile. "This whole…" he waved a finger between the pair of them "…whatever it was…*is*…it's uncharted territory for me. And it's certainly not 'slumming it,' as you so elegantly put it." His voice took on an edge. "Don't treat yourself that way, Cailey. It's not how I think of you and it certainly isn't how you should think about yourself."

His admonishment silenced her. Just as well, considering he was sucking in another breath for part two.

"The point is, however great last night was, children are definitely not on the cards for me—and I'm guessing they're not for you either, with your big-city lifestyle. You're focusing on your career. I'm trying to keep the clinic afloat. So…" He gave his hands one of those *here-goes-nothing* claps. "We'll get you the pill and everything'll be sorted. By tonight it'll be as if the whole thing never happened."

He gave her a solid nod, as if that was the end of that. Something in her bridled. As if it had *never happened*? Seriously? *That* was how much last night had meant to him?

What a Class-A wazzock he was being—as one of the nurses in London liked to say. She wasn't a hundred percent sure what it meant, but it didn't sound good. Not that *she* was much better, though.

She was an idiot to have thought last night was anything other than just a life-affirming connection in the wake of a crisis. Sure, they'd both worked their guts out. And, yes, working together had been as organic as if they'd been doing it all their lives. But she was the only one who had dreamt of being with Theo. That much was clear.

He wanted to forget all about it? *Fine*. Two could play at that game.

"Thanks so much for the coffee," she said with a saccharine smile. "It was lovely."

She took a step forward, a bit annoyed there wasn't enough room in the corridor to swish past him. There wasn't a chance in hell—or on earth either, for that matter—that she was going to cry in front of him.

"Glad you liked it."

Theo put his mug down on a small table and clapped his hands on her shoulders. It wasn't sexy. Definitely more older brother to kid sister than lover to lover.

Why couldn't he just move, so she could finally exhale the epic sigh trapped in her lungs?

The little flicker of hope he'd lit when he'd appeared with the coffee and a sort of apology was completely and utterly tamped out. It had been one night. One amazing, sensual, madcap, lusty night, to be lodged in her memory banks forever.

"We'll sort this out at the clinic, yeah? I'll meet you there in ten...maybe twenty minutes. I have a couple of phone calls I'd like to make beforehand. Just introduce yourself to whoever's on duty and they'll sort you out. I'm sure the overnight crews will be desperate to get some sleep."

She stared at him. Really? That was it? *Thanks for the sex, glad you liked your coffee, now beat it?*

He blinked, then looked away.

Oh, yeah. That flicker of hope was well and truly extinguished. He was probably going to call Dimitri. Get him to call out the cavalry to herd her off the island.

She turned on her heel and left. No chance, no way, no how was she going to let Theo Nikolaides crush her heart all over again. She was going to go back to that clinic and show him what he was really missing.

Then she'd leave. On *her* terms.

"Cailey!"

Theo called out her name a second time, but the heavy slam of the door drowned out his voice.

Fix it, man! Bloody *fix* it.

He punched the wall, instantly regretting it. What the hell was a fist going to do to a wall that had withstood a few centuries, not to mention an epic earthquake? And since when did he take things out on stationary objects?

What a terrible mess.

He liked Cailey. Always had. Seeing her again had reawoken something in him he'd never really put a name to. Something beyond desire.

He scrubbed a hand through his hair. What an idiot. For a doctor he really could be oblivious sometimes. From the moment she'd appeared at the clinic it was if…as if he'd been made whole.

Typical.

The answer both to his dreams and his worst ever nightmare was all wrapped up in the same dark-eyed, black-haired, sensual, kind-hearted package.

He'd handled things with Cailey about as well as he'd handled Dimitri when push had come to shove. The day he'd told his adoptive father he'd have to make a choice. Show him some respect or face the consequences.

He'd well and truly thought Dimitri would choose the latter.

That showdown had been the single most terrifying and empowering moment of his life.

He pressed his thumbs to his eyes as if it would erase the memories, but until he drew his last breath he would remember each second of that day to within a particle of its essence.

His sister had just been unceremoniously shipped off to boarding school in England and tensions had been simmering between him and his father ever since.

"Why not just man up and do what you've been bred to do?" his father had roared when Theo had come to him with a proposal.

"What? Like a stallion?" Theo had retorted, drawing himself to the fullest height his nine-teen-year-old self had allowed. "A bull? Is *that* why you pulled me off the streets? To ensure the Nikolaides line continues exactly as you imagine? Three-piece suits, an heiress of your choice for a bride and lording it over the rest of Mythelios as if I were amongst the Chosen Ones?"

He'd run his eyes the length of his father, unable to conceal his contempt.

"Not a chance in hell."

His father's eyes had narrowed and crackled with a deep anger Theo had never seen flare so bright. This fight wasn't their usual flare-up over some trivial social gaffe—Theo wearing the wrong outfit, saying the wrong thing, shaking the wrong hand, pouring the wrong cocktail. This one had begun over the dream Theo had shared with his best mates: to become an island doctor at a clinic they would create to fill the void now the state-run hospital had reluctantly closed its doors.

He'd thought he'd made all the right steps. He'd had perfect grades. The best manners. And, as his father had hoped, Theo had forged deep and lasting friendships with the sons of Dimitri's business partners...the four men who'd had an idea for a local Greek shipping company and turned it into a global phenomenon: Mopaxeni Shipping.

Their wealth had surpassed all their expectations. But it hadn't changed who they were at heart—and that day Theo had learned who his adopted father really was.

A man so fearful of losing his status he

would go to any limits to keep it. He'd grown up poor. He'd known hunger. He'd known loss. He'd endured fear and pain. And he'd vowed never to feel any of those things ever again.

Being forced to adopt a child had been a critical blow to his ego. A virile, powerful man, unable to impregnate his own wife? A billionaire powerless to have a son of his own?

He'd solved the problem by literally buying Theo from an orphanage. Money meant privacy. No paper trail to expose Dimitri's one weak point.

And then had come Erianthe. The miracle baby. Perhaps his adoptive mother had felt less stress to "produce" after they'd adopted Theo. Perhaps Dimitri had. Either way—they'd had their own child and Dimitri had never lost an opportunity to remind Theo of just how lucky he'd been to be adopted by a wealthy man.

When Theo had asked to use his trust fund to establish the Mythelios Free Clinic his father had actually laughed.

"That's no sort of business," he'd howled, virtually wiping away tears of disbelief. "You *do* understand what the word 'non-profit' means, don't you, Theo?"

"I understand that Mythelios has no physician. No hospital."

"No son of *mine* will become a common island doctor. It's no better than being a vegetable merchant or a mechanic!"

"And what's wrong with that?" Theo had countered. "Who fixes your car when it breaks? Who feeds you? Who grows the food you eat? Clothes you? Cleans your house? *People!* Living, breathing people, with hearts beating in their chests!"

"What do I care for other people's hearts?"

"Nothing, from what I can see!" Theo had spat in response.

His father had moved as if to hit him.

Theo had caught his wrist tight and said, in no uncertain terms, "If you continue down this path, one by one the people of Mythelios will come forward and tell you to your face just how little they respect you."

"The people of Mythelios *do* respect me." Dimitri had growled, his fist still encased in his son's palm. If there was one thing Dimitri prized more than money it was respect.

"*Do* they?" Theo had dropped his hold. "You can't *buy* respect. Or loyalty. Those things have to be earned. Tell me…was it Spiro, a humble plumber, who became mayor, or you? What about the island's public service awards? Are any of those plaques hanging on *your* walls?"

The questions were rhetorical and they both knew it.

His father had turned white with rage. So Theo had reached out an olive branch. The point of their discussion hadn't been for his father to suffer. He'd just wanted Dimitri to feel compassion. Some innate empathy for those less driven to increase his bank account. But more than anything he'd wanted the man who had given him so many opportunities to be proud of the path he'd chosen.

"Funding a clinic to help people who began life just as you did—with only the dreams in their hearts—would go a long way to improving that precious public image of yours," Theo had declared.

So they'd agreed.

Once Theo was qualified Dimitri would give him the money to start up the clinic, and in turn Theo would laud his father for his largesse. After that Theo's trust fund—and those of his three friends—would be enough to keep it going. In short, it would be a business agreement disguised as familial love—and it had worked, even if Theo had thrown every penny he had at it, leaving little over for himself.

The jangle of Theo's phone broke through the wash of memories threatening to consume him. He pulled the handset out of the trousers he'd discarded the night before and stared at the screen.

Erianthe. She had a second sense, that one. Always knew when he needed a dose of real love. Loving his sister seemed to be the only thing that came naturally to him. Maybe because it had always been protective. Protecting her from Dimitri's rages. From her own tempestuous ways. Boarding school seemed to have done the same thing to her as it had to him. Focused her drive and ambition.

"Eri *mou!*"

"Hey, big brother. How's my island? Still holding together with sticky tape and a bit of elbow grease?"

Despite himself, he laughed. She'd called yesterday and asked the exact same thing. It wasn't entitlement in her case. It was her heart. She was a true Mythelonian. So he repeated what he'd said yesterday. "We're managing. Stay where you are and finish getting that medical degree. *Then* you're allowed to come home."

"Thanks, Mr. Bossy."

"Hey! Big brother knows best." He tried to tack on a laugh, but he wasn't feeling it. Not today. He just felt…bossy.

"It feels pathetic to stay here while you're shouldering the load," Erianthe play-protested. She knew she was just a couple of months away from getting her specialist degree. Dropping it now would be a fool's errand.

"Don't worry. The lads are coming in soon."

He looked round for his coffee mug, found it and took a fortifying swig, relieved to be able to think about work again. Much safer territory.

"All of them?"

He thought he heard a note of anxiety in her voice but dismissed it. With him, she was a straight talker. If she wanted to ask something, she asked.

"Yup. We've got quite a few relief doctors in from Athens until they can come. Chris is coming as soon as his contract ends. Two or three weeks from now. Deakin…not sure, exactly. I think he's stuck in New York for a couple of months but he has promised to do a stint."

"Anyone else?" Her voice was quiet and a little strange.

"Not sure. I've been trying to get hold of Ares, but you know him. International Man of Mystery and Medicine. I can't locate him. I think he might be in Africa somewhere, but he tends to be where mobile telephone signals are *not*."

"Oh. Good. Fine."

Now her voice sounded strangely bright. Since she'd passed through her teens Erianthe didn't really *do* emotional, so the happier she sounded, the more worried she usually was.

"It *is* fine, sis. Everyone's fine. Why did you ring?"

"Just to check up. I tried talking with Mum and Dad and that went about as well as expected."

Theo huffed a mirthless laugh. "I heard he had his driver take him on a tour of the destruction yesterday. Still haven't heard if he plans to help anyone."

"I thought that was *your* job?" Erianthe parried.

Yes. Well. He supposed it was. Dimitri earned the money. Theo wrestled some of it out of him to do good. That was how they rolled. One big happy do-gooding family.

"Hey! You'll never guess who turned up yesterday." Now it was *his* turn to sound unnaturally chit-chatty. "Cailey Tomaras."

"Cailey?" Erianthe whooped. "That's great. I haven't heard from her in years. Is she well?"

"Didn't you two stay in touch while you were at boarding school?"

"Nope."

"Why not?"

"Dad."

Ah. Enough said, he thought with a mental eye-roll. Dad's money, Dad's rules.

"How is she?" Erianthe asked. "Did she ever get into med school?"

"Med school? No. She's a nurse. Neonatal. She works in some fancy maternity hospital in London."

"Oh. I never realized she was so close or I would have got in touch. But that's funny... She always told me she wanted to be a doctor. Guess she got smart and figured out a much faster route to helping people was to become a nurse."

"Not long now and you'll be doing just the same, Eri."

He smiled as his sister gave a melodramatic sigh. "I know... I just wish... I just wish I was there now with you. Helping."

"You will be. Soon. Now hang up the phone and let me get to work, okay?"

"Okay. Love you."

"Love you, too."

He stared at the phone as he disconnected the call, wondering if he'd ever hear those words from his father.

Maybe not.

Just as he'd never say the words to a child of his own. Too much history to inflict on an innocent. Too many conditions.

He stopped himself punching the wall again. He hated that what had happened between Cailey and him had been slashed in two by a foolish oversight. Chances were slim to nil she'd ever want to speak with him again.

But perhaps it was best to have it all nipped in the bud now. The day he'd bullied that money from Dimitri was the day he'd vowed never to trust himself as a father. And Cailey deserved to live the life she wanted. Not walk the tightrope of conditional love he'd chosen for himself.

CHAPTER TEN

"HELENA FAIRFAX?" CAILEY called out the name, scanning the crowd for a hint of recognition. Though it was still early morning, the crowd at the clinic had grown.

"Here!" an English voice called out, and Cailey caught sight of a hand waving above the sea of heads clustered in the reception area. "Here, it's me!"

The crowd shifted and moved as the woman worked her way forward. Cailey had to stop herself from gawping when the woman emerged from the crowd.

"Mrs. Fairfax?"

The woman nodded, gingerly holding a barbecue fork inside her mouth…its tines visible on the outside of her cheek, "Dat's me!" Incredibly, she managed to smile. "I didn't know if I should try to pull it out," she mumbled around the utensil. "Thought I might leave that bit to you."

For all of the things she *didn't* love about the British, Cailey certainly loved their pluck! She didn't think *she'd* be smiling under the same set of circumstances.

"Good. Smart thinking." Cailey held her arms wide to show Helena where to go. "Let's take a look at that in an exam room, shall we?"

"I see you've begun without me."

Cailey's spine shot ramrod-straight at the sound of Theo's voice. *Terrific.* Just what she needed. Theo's presence had felt reassuring yesterday. And now, just a few hours of love-making later, it felt…really, really unnerving. He boss. She underling. He man… She frail woman who just might be pregnant.

How could he sound so…so calm, cool and collected after what had happened?

She might be carrying his child, for heaven's sake! Okay. So it wasn't a baby just yet. Biologically speaking she knew that would take a day or so…or maybe not happen at all…but—

"Nurse Tomaras? Any chance you're going to take Mrs. Fairfax into an exam room?"

"Why, yes…" she ground out.

So it was *Nurse Tomaras* now, was it?

"There most certainly is, *Dr.* Nikolaides." She smiled warmly at Helena. "Please. Do follow me."

She showed her to a curtained area at the

far end of the bustling clinic and settled Helena onto the exam table before pulling a bright light round—all of which she did without giving "Dr. Nikolaides" so much as a glance.

Puncture wounds were mostly tricky if they were near organs or key arteries. Luckily the cheek was a relatively safe area in so far as acute damage was concerned.

Cailey snapped on a pair of hygienic gloves hard enough to sting, which served only to irritate her more as she pulled up a wheelie stool to take a better look. She glanced at Theo, who had just finished pulling the curtains around the cubicle.

"I'm just taking a look. Unless you'd like to examine the patient first, *Doctor*?"

"Um…" Helena flicked her eyes between the pair. "Is everything all right between you two?"

"Perfect!"

"Couldn't be better."

They glared at one another as their words overlapped.

Cailey knew she shouldn't be angry. Taking the morning-after pill was a perfectly acceptable solution to their dilemma—she just wished he hadn't gone so…so Robot Man on her. It wasn't as if she'd been trying to trap him, or anything.

Sternly she reminded herself that she shouldn't put words in his mouth. He hadn't said anything of the sort. He'd been perfectly civil.

"Would you *like* me to take a look?" he asked, more mildly.

She glared him again, and then pushed her stool backwards. It wasn't as if she had a vast amount of experience in pulling barbecue forks out of women's faces.

Theo put his hands on his knees, readjusted the light and took a look. "Well, the good news is it doesn't look like there's any structural damage to your cheek. Puncture wounds, if kept clean, are pretty good healers, so you won't need stitches. But before— Whoops!"

The wheels of the supplies trolley Cailey had been preparing started to slide across the floor as another aftershock hit.

"No!"

Theo was falling toward Helena and Cailey leapt behind him and pulled him back, furious with herself for enjoying the feeling of his tight bum pressed against her. Last night she would have given her hips a bit of a shift and grind. If there wasn't a patient in front of him now...

"Oops!"

Cailey lost her balance and Helena yelped as Theo's hand bumped against the fork handle as the aftershock sent the pair of them tumbling to the floor.

"Sorry! *Sorry!* Aftershock."

Cailey scrambled to her feet, cheeks streaked pink with embarrassment. She'd landed right on top of Theo and for a split second had considered kissing his Adam's apple.

Helena rolled her eyes. The woman was clearly made of stern stuff. Or else she thought the two of them were completely insane.

After Theo had levered himself back up and shot Cailey a peculiar look, he moved the light again and took a good look. "I heard on the way in they're going to get the electricity back on soon, so you won't have to barbecue your breakfast for much longer."

Even Cailey laughed at that. Staying grumpy around a man who embodied the word *congenial* was tough. Not to mention a man who was funny, kind, an excellent doctor and stupidly gorgeous.

But other than that…? Total. Jerk.

"Thank you so much, Dr. Nikolaides. You're a star."

And he had been. After a numbing agent haad been administered in one swift, effortless move he had released the fork.

Helena didn't mention the exacting care with which Cailey had applied the small bandage over the two perfect tine marks. It was all, Theo, Theo, Theo.

"Serves me right for being such a greedy cow!" Helena laughed. Flirtatiously. As if she wasn't married. Which she clearly was. A rock the size of marble flashed on her finger.

Theo, who was washing his hands at the sink, shot the patient an amused look. "Oh?"

"There was a bit of sausage left on the fork and I decided I'd gobble it up before my husband and the boys saw it, but then an aftershock hit. *Ooh!*" She gingerly pressed her hand to her cheek. "Talking too much should probably be off the menu."

"Right, *Mrs.* Fairfax." Cailey indicated that she could get off the exam table. "Take the bandage off after half an hour or so. It's just there to catch anything we haven't managed to tidy up. I know it seems counterintuitive, but it's actually better for puncture wounds to let them breathe."

"Nothing like the fresh salty air of Mythelios to help heal me!"

"Is this your first time here?" Theo asked, clearly enjoying his patient's obvious coquettish looks.

You'd think he would be a bit more concerned about the queue of patients waiting out there.

"Not at all. We're from Britain," she said, in her cut-glass accent. "Obviously."

"Not tempted to go home, given the quake?"

"Not yet! We've got a jolly good tale to take home. This place is like a second home to us. Been coming for years. My husband and I had our first…well…" She feigned embarrassment, fluttered her lashes, then lowered her voice to a sultry bedroom tone. "We had our first proper assignation here."

Cailey's cheeks instantly flared with heat. Good grief! They'd asked for the woman's medical history, not a blow-by-blow account of her sex life!

"The island does that to people," Theo replied factually, before latching eyes with Cailey.

Her heart skipped a beat. *Maybe…*

"All right then, Mrs. Fairfax." Theo returned his attention to the patient. "Do let us know if the wound starts to feel anything out of the ordinary. Heat. Tingling. You'll want to do your best to prevent infection. But we like to try and avoid antibiotics if we can."

"Oh! Heavens. Don't worry about anything like that. I'll keep it clean. Do a little saltwater gargle every few hours or so. Ta-ta for now!"

And with that she scooped up her handbag, swirled past the curtains and was gone.

"Right, then, Nurse Tomaras." Theo closed the door behind him and turned around to face her.

"Please don't call me that." Cailey scowled. "I think it's probably fair to suggest we're on a first-name basis by now."

He arched an eyebrow at her.

She tried to arch one back and failed, so turned around and started cleaning up everything from Mrs. Fairfax's treatment instead.

Cleaning, her mother had always insisted, was a cure-all.

"Cailey. Can you stop that for a minute?"

"Not really, no. It needs to be tidied and there are loads of patients out there waiting. Maybe you can make yourself useful by asking Petra who's up next?"

"Not until you stop disinfecting everything in sight and look at me."

He wasn't enjoying this any more than she was. And probably found talking about it twice as hard.

She pointedly laid down the spray bottle and shoved the paper toweling she'd been using into the bin, put her hands on her hips and gave him her best attentive face.

"I thought you might want this." He dug into his pocket and pulled out the single tablet encased in garish bright orange plastic packaging. "Subtle, huh?"

He laughed, but his words fell between them like lead. It wasn't funny. And he wasn't handling this well. Surprise, surprise. His bedside manner only seemed to come to him when a patient was actually a patient.

Cailey's hand snapped out to grab the packet. He held it up out of her reach.

"Seriously? C'mon, Theo. Just hand it over."

"You don't look very happy about it."

"I'm not."

"Why not?"

"It's just…it…" She huffed out an exasperated sigh. "It's hardly the stuff of romance, is it?"

"So it's a lack of romance that you're worried about rather than having a baby?"

Nice one, mate. Way to show Cailey support.

"So far, according to my humble nursing classes, there *is* no baby. This little pill will just make certain of it."

She snatched the orange rectangle from him, stuffed it in her pocket and looked up at him with defiance written across her features.

"Happy? Can I get back to work now?"

"No. And no. Not until we talk about this."

"What's there to talk about?" she whispered angrily. "We had a one-night stand. It was just about the sexiest thing that's ever happened to me in my entire life and now it's over. So, if you would kindly leave me to it, *Dr.* Nikolaides, there's a rather large crowd gathered outside hoping for some medical treatment."

"Cailey, if you don't want to take that pill, don't take it."

Her hands shifted from balled-up fists on her hips to a protective criss-crossing over her chest.

"And what? You'll suddenly discover a deep-seated desire for a picket fence lifestyle and become a father to a baby we don't even know exists? Yeah. I don't think so."

Her entire body radiated defensiveness. A reaction, no doubt, to his clinical approach— which was only making this bad situation about a thousand times worse.

"You're right." He forced himself to keep his voice low and steady. His father's would be up at about nine decibels by now.

The cubicle curtain was hardly soundproof, and if there was one thing he valued it was privacy. Honesty was on a par with that.

"If you'll forgive my bluntness, a child is the last thing I want. Cailey— Oh, please don't cry…here."

He pulled a tissue out of the box on the supplies trolley and handed it to her. He should pull her to him. Hold her until the tears stopped. Kiss her until the fear abated. But he wasn't built that way. Wasn't equipped to absorb her fears. Stark evidence, if he needed any, that he didn't have what it took to be a father.

But he wasn't having her run out into the clinic with tears pouring down her face either. Facing up to his father had, at the very least, given him the courage to face situations head-on.

He tipped his head toward the exam table. "C'mon. Take a seat."

"There are *patients* waiting, Doctor," Cailey growled, swiping furiously at the tears escaping from her eyes.

"Yes. And they're going to have to wait for two more minutes. The trauma team is fully staffed. *You're* what's important right now."

She shot him a dubious look as she hoisted herself up onto the exam table. "And how exactly do you come to that conclusion, Dr. Nikolaides?"

"Well, *Cailey*…as you noted earlier, I think we're on an intimate enough basis that we can go with first names from here on out—yes?"

She nodded and reached across to grab more tissues, but not before throwing him another dark look.

"Right." He sat on the exam table beside

her. "I think we can both agree neither of us is happy with this solution." He pointed to the pocket where she'd put the pill.

"Look who got the high scores in med school!" Cailey poked him in the thigh with an index finger.

He took solace from her stab at black humor. "I work all the time. Your life is in London. So, I think we can also agree we're not really in the best place to have a baby."

"Just like that?"

She didn't want *a child now, did she?*

"I thought you wanted to focus on your career. That sort of commitment takes time. Time you won't have if you have a child."

"We don't even know if I'm pregnant yet, Theo!"

"So what are you saying? Do you want to wait and find out if you are and *then* make a decision?"

"No." There wasn't the slightest hint of a waver in her answer.

"What, then? Tell me what you want."

She glared at him, her face a picture of resilience and strength—before her features crumbled and a solitary tear snaked down her cheek.

"Just… I'll take the pill and in a few days, when you don't need me anymore—when the *clinic* doesn't need me anymore—I'll go back to my 'big-city life', as you call it, and you'll never have to think about me again."

"Cailey. *Koukla mou*." He swept away the tear with the pad of his thumb. "That would be impossible."

She sniffed and batted his hands away. "It's not exactly as if you're offering a red carpet invitation to stay on the island and see what would happen if—" She sucked in a big breath and pressed her fist to her mouth.

"If what?"

She shook her head. She wasn't going to answer, but instinct allowed him to fill in the blanks. She meant see what would happen between them if she lived here. If they dated. If they went about their lives like all sorts of other young couples did—exploring the possibilities of love.

Damn. This was one area he couldn't go.

His phone buzzed in his pocket. He tugged it out and looked at the screen. A message from his father.

Dinner. Tonight. Nine p.m.

Typical Dimitri message. Commands. All the man did was tell people what to do.

Precisely what he *was doing with Cailey.*

"Why don't you sleep on it?"

"What?" Cailey looked at him as if he'd just pulled magic pine cones out of his ears.

"Sleep on it. You have time." He took her hand in his. "*We* have time."

Her palm lay limp in his and she said nothing, so he continued.

"You can take the pill anytime in the next seventy-two hours. That gives you—"

"Three days," Cailey completed for him. "I know. I may not be a doctor, but even a nurse knows how this medicine works."

Theo's eyes widened. "I wasn't suggesting—"

"Yeah. I know. A good nurse is like gold dust," she recited in a monotone voice as she gave her hair a shake, pulled an elastic band out of her pocket and bundled her curls into submission.

"Cailey." He bent down and picked up the pill packet that had fallen out of her pocket when she'd retrieved her hairband. When he handed it to her again their eyes caught and locked tight. A jolt of invisible electricity crackled between them as their fingers touched.

He closed his eyes against it and sighed. What a mess. If only he'd been raised by a normal, loving family he might have the skills to deal with this better. Or if Cailey were a patient... Patients were easy. In the door—out the door. A few minutes of understanding, advising and then they were gone. Nothing personal…nothing lasting.

When he opened his eyes again Cailey's entire demeanor had turned prickly again.

"So…" She pushed the packet back into her pocket and straightened her scrubs top. "What do we do in between?"

"You mean for the next seventy-hours? Well… We could behave like ten-year-olds and pretend we don't know each other, or we could just carry on as we did yesterday."

Cailey's eyes widened.

"Working together."

"Ah. Yes. Good. And I'm totally looking forward to sleeping on my mum's sofa."

"There's always my spare room—"

"Nope! *No*. No, thank you. I am all about the sofa." She gave him a grim smile and hopped off the exam table.

A wave of protectiveness swept through him. As insane as it seemed, this scare made him want to spend *more* time with her, not less. And yet he knew intimacy, love without conditions, selflessness…those weren't skills he had in his arsenal.

He got down off the exam table too, and did a few boxing moves. Cailey's bewildered expression had told him all he needed to know.

Handling anything more intimate than a one-night stand was definitely *not* his forte.

"We're in this together, right, buddy?" he said. *Buddy?*

"Yeah…" Cailey took a step back, grabbed her stethoscope from the supplies tray and yoked it round her neck. "Whatever you say, Doctor."

Then she whipped open the cubicle curtain and headed to Reception to find their next patient.

CHAPTER ELEVEN

"You sure you've had enough to eat?"

Cailey pulled her mother into a tight hug. "Yes, Mama. I've had enough for two!"

The second the words were out of her mouth she realized just how right she might be.

The pill.

It was two weeks since Theo had given it to her…and she had completely forgotten to take it. No doubt he assumed she'd done the sensible thing and had taken it.

It seemed sheer madness that something so huge had simply slipped her mind. She hadn't thought of anything else for the first couple of days. Each time it had popped into her mind she'd tried to reasonably weigh out the pros and cons. Then the enormity of the decision would begin to engulf any sort of common sense she had, so she'd give herself a couple more hours to think about it.

She'd decided to prioritize. The first thing

she needed to do was block Theo from her radar. Forcing herself to remember the day Dimitri Nikolaides had made it more than clear that she would never be good enough for his son was all she'd needed to do to start burying her feelings for him. She'd done it once, she reasoned, and she could do it again.

But last time she hadn't made love to him. Last time there hadn't been the slightest chance she was carrying his child.

Oh, no, no, no. This wasn't happening. This couldn't be happening!

Things had been so busy at the clinic she'd barely seen Theo, let alone spoken to him. And the doctor she'd been working with instead, Alex Balaban, had proved to be a much-needed distraction from her problems. He worked at a teaching hospital in Athens, and clearly loved sharing his years of experience with anyone who would listen—unlike many of the doctors she'd encountered, who thought nurses were merely there to tidy up and wipe away a patient's tears.

Dr. Balaban had sensed her eagerness to learn and over the past two weeks…had it been a *fortnight* already?… Cailey had been completely consumed with learning, helping, and caring for each of the patients who came through the clinic doors. If Theo didn't want her, the patients certainly did.

Popo! How *could* she have forgotten something so important?

"Cailey *mou*! My love. Let your mother breathe!"

Cailey instantly dropped her arms, whipped around and grabbed her backpack off the freshly tidied sofa. She made a big show of finding her trainers, getting just the right pair of socks. *Busy.* She needed to keep busy until she could wrap her head around this.

"Do you want me to do some laundry for you today?" her mother asked, in a voice that actually meant, *What are you hiding from me?*

She could feel her mother's eyes burning holes in the back of her head. Or perhaps it was her own guilt for keeping something so huge from her mother. Not that her mother had questioned Cailey when she'd told her she'd decided the sofa was fine, as Theo was now hosting a load of the visiting doctors from Athens at his house.

She'd raised a dubious eyebrow but she hadn't pressed. Softly, softly was her mother's technique, and usually…always…it worked in the end.

"No, Mama. That's fine. I'll do it when I get home. To London," she qualified.

"What? Leaving so soon?"

The fact that she hadn't jumped on a plane the same day Theo had handed her the morning-after pill had been a minor miracle, but things had truly been busy at the clinic, and when she'd suggested she assist one of the out-of-town doctors, seeing as she knew most of the locals, Theo had put up scant resistance.

"Things are slowing down at the clinic. I think some of the volunteers from Athens will be heading back soon. I'm sure they don't need a lowly nurse clogging things up once the Mopaxeni lads start coming in."

"Cailey!"

Her mother's tone was so sharp she turned to face her.

"Don't you *dare* speak of your achievements in that way."

"Being a nurse wasn't exactly my original plan, though, was it?"

"And being a housekeeper wasn't mine," her mother reprimanded. "I planned to be an astronaut. Did you know that?" She smiled, her eyes flicking out the window and up to the cloudless sky. "We may not always get what we think we want, but we usually get what we need."

Cailey bit down on the inside of her cheek. Hard enough to draw blood. Her mother rarely played the "fisherman's widow" card. Or the "housekeeper to an ungrateful billionaire" card. Her mother was grace personified. And the reminder of all her mother had lost and fought for humbled her.

"I'm sorry, Mama."

"There's absolutely nothing to be sorry for, Cailey. And remember I am *proud* of the work I did for Mr. Nikolaides. I am even more proud of you and your brothers. You've soared beyond anything I hoped for you."

"What *did* you hope for us?" Cailey had never asked. She supposed she'd always been too busy being wrapped up in what she *didn't* have to think about what she did.

Her mother looked her square in the eye. "I wanted you to be healthy. And I wanted you to be happy."

"What if I would've been happier if I was a doctor?"

"*Would* you? It would mean you'd still be in some university somewhere now. It would mean all those children you've helped bring into the world would not have had you to clean them, swaddle them, give them a goodnight kiss. It would mean you wouldn't have been able to help all the people here these past two weeks."

Cailey tipped her head back and took a deep breath.

"You *tried*, love," her mother continued. "You tried with every ounce of your being to get into medical school. Is it fair you didn't get in? Probably not. Is it fair we didn't have enough money for special tutors or private schools or whatever else might have helped you with your dyslexia? Absolutely not. But you are a wonderful nurse, at an incredible hospital, and I bet each and every one of your patients thinks the world of you."

"If I was a doctor I'd be able to afford to give you back the money you lent me for nursing school and you could get a bigger place."

"What makes you think I don't love it here in my flat?"

"Well…it's—"

"It's absolutely perfect. I spent my entire life cleaning up after you and the Nikolaideses—and took pride in it," she added, before Cailey could jump in. "But now that I'm retired I'm loving looking after just me. I barely have to dust. There is no silver to polish. No chandelier crystals to wash. It's perfect. I'm happy. And all I want now is to make sure you are, too."

Cailey opened her mouth to say that of course she was happy, but nothing came out. Coming home had opened up her very own Pandora's box of insecurities and they seemed to be flying at her like a swarm of locusts.

Theo.

Being in his arms and then being pushed away in a matter of hours.

Unprotected sex.

It all proved yet again that she wasn't worthy of being a Nikolaides bride—because who behaved this recklessly?

Worthy? What was *worthy* at the end of the day?

She'd carried more than one baby out of the arms of a mother who'd opted to give her child away rather than take on the responsibility of parenthood herself. Were those women unworthy or were they just scared? Had they been rejected at some point themselves?

She understood the soul-destroying path of self-destruction that could lead to. She thought she'd tackled the way the Nikolaides family had made her feel. Got back up on her feet and made something of herself. But now…

Now she felt as though she'd been split into two very distinct parts. The pragmatic part that was wishing for a time machine. She should have ripped open that packet in front of Theo and swallowed the pill there and then. Problem solved. And the other part of her…the huge thumping, powerful ache in her heart…was utterly relieved she had done no such thing.

"You're right, Mama. I'm sorry."

"No." Her mother cupped her face in her hand. "Don't apologize for being human. Just promise me you'll look after this big heart of yours, all right?" She put her other hand on Cailey's sternum. "Listen to it. It's wiser than you give it credit for."

Cailey nodded and gave her mother a quick, tight squeeze. "Well, I guess I'd better go see some patients. Doctors are absolutely useless without a good nurse backing them up."

"That's my girl."

Her mother gave her a quick kiss, handed her a bag filled with homemade almond biscuits and shooed her out the door.

The clinic was strangely quiet when she entered.

There were a few patients waiting in the trauma section and the general reception area, but there didn't seem to be as many staff scurrying around.

Then she heard the motor of a boat shift into low gear at the back of the clinic.

Petra spied her from the central reception desk and pointed toward the dock area. "New patient coming in. Out you go!"

Cailey couldn't help but smile as she obeyed. Petra ran the clinic as if it were her own. What she said went. So Cailey scuttled out through the back door and on to the short pier, where a fisherman was pulling up in his boat. There wasn't any official ambulance vessel, so the local fishermen had been bringing in anyone they could if it meant a shorter trip for the patients.

As the forty-something man threw his rope toward the dock she caught it and smiled. Though her memories of her father were hazy, the ruddy complexions and bulging muscles of the men commanding this particular boat reminded her of him. She'd thought he was the most powerful man in the world, and when her mother had told her the sea had taken him…

It had been a profound reminder of how precious life was, and that each rescued soul represented a triumph against Mother Nature's might.

She knelt and secured the rope to the dock cleat, just as her father had taught her. If she was pregnant she'd teach her child just as her father had taught her… First one swoop of the rope—

"Cailey?"

She whipped round at the sound of Theo's voice. How he still managed to take her breath away when he'd been nothing but the consummate, cool professional over the past couple of weeks was beyond her.

Pffft. No, it wasn't. She'd been told to stay away from him years ago. And she had. But those years apart hadn't made the slightest bit of difference. In the very first moment they'd laid eyes on each either other again a love that had never died had blossomed once more in her heart.

Her hands instinctively swept to her stomach. She'd have to tell him. But how?

"Are you up to date on what's happened to these patients?" Theo asked, all business.

"No, Petra just said to come out here. Is Dr. Balaban on his way?"

Theo shook his head. "He went off with the fire crew."

"Is Kyros all right?"

"Yes, he was driving the rig, I think. It's a house fire. Someone moving in before the gas company had a chance to check the lines and—" He made the sound of an explosion, mimicking the incident with his hands.

"Bad?" She couldn't hide her wince. Burn patients suffered so deeply.

"We'll know soon enough. They're going to try to bring them back here and treat them. No choppers to Athens for a few more hours. Until then you're with me."

Before she could react one of the fisherman was helping a young boy wearing a backpack step across to the pier. When he put his hand on the boy's elbow the boy screamed in pain.

Theo, with a complete lack of self-consciousness, quickly took the boy's right hand in his. "Cailey, meet Nicolas. Nicolas, meet the best nurse Mythelios has on offer." Theo glanced down at the boy's other hand and sucked in a sharp breath.

"She'd better have the patience of a saint!" A heavily pregnant woman held out a hand for Cailey to help her off the boat.

"And this is Nicolas's mum—Georgia Stephanopolous."

"Nicolas shouldn't be taking up your time," Georgia snapped, her features taut with distress. "Not when there is so much else going on."

Cailey gave Georgia a nod of acknowledgement, then looked at Nicolas. The boy's hangdog expression had grown even deeper.

"Perhaps *you* can knock some sense into him," she said when she caught Cailey's confused expression.

"It was an accident!" The boy looked up at her with wide, pleading eyes.

All other thoughts dropped away as Cailey absorbed the scene. Tense mother. Young son—maybe six? Seven years old? He was wearing a backpack. He had scraped knees.

And what was that stuck in his hand? It looked like *needles* of some sort.

She looked to Theo to explain as they all began walking to the clinic.

"So, Nicolas here was being a bit of a hero—"

"A bit of a *fool*!" his mother interjected.

Theo didn't respond to the comment so Cailey followed his lead. When parents were distressed their fear often manifested itself as anger. Rage, even. Any comment made to placate or suggest otherwise was often adding fuel to the fire. A hurt child was already a tense situation.

"Nicolas," continued Theo, in a strong, steady voice, "was trying to rescue a kitten that had been trapped in some rubble, and he managed not only to dislocate his elbow, but also fell into his mother's cactus garden in the process. Bad luck, little chap." He tousled the boy's hair and gave him a smile.

Poor kid. Cailey gave his thin shoulder a squeeze. A sting of sadness seared her heart when tears appeared in his eyes. "Did you manage to rescue the kitten?"

The little boy nodded, fat tears plopping out onto his cheeks and rolling through the streaks of dust he'd acquired during the rescue. "His name is Zeus," he whispered, his shoulders hunching against the anticipated response from his mother as they all went into the exam room.

Cailey closed the door, seeing Georgia's eye-roll, and then, unexpectedly, the woman burst into tears.

"Zeus is his father's name," she sobbed.

Cailey threw Theo a bewildered look. He calmly handed her a box of tissues, lifted Nicolas up to the exam table and nodded at Cailey to go with her instincts and give the poor woman a hug.

"That's a *good* thing, right?"

"No!" Georgia wailed, her body dissolving into shudders and low moans which had the knock-on effect of eliciting a fresh wash of tears from her son.

Cailey held the woman as tightly as she could and looked over her shoulder at Theo, mouthing, *What happened?*

Theo made a quick check to see if Nicolas was looking. His big brown eyes were solidly focused on his feet, swinging limply from the exam table. Then Theo looked grave and shook his head.

The minute gesture spoke volumes.

Nicolas's father had been killed in the quake.

Blackness shrouded her heart as the weight of the revelation pressed the air from her lungs. She knew exactly how this little boy felt, and for the first time she was getting a glimpse of how incredibly brave and strong her mother must have been in the wake of her own father's death.

Seeing the situation from an adult perspective—as a cruel, senseless death—instantly deepened the love she had for her mother.

As Cailey held Georgia in a tight hug she watched as Theo talked the boy through each of the steps he was taking. A quick injection for pain relief. Then they would get to the elbow as soon as he had plucked the evil-looking cactus barbs from his hand. Not that Theo *said* they were evil. Instead he used words to describe Nicolas like "brave" and "strong" and "selfless."

All words she could use to describe Theo.

How could a man this amazing not want a child of his own?

She concentrated on the weight Nicolas's mother was letting her accept as she wept and grieved. When Cailey had first seen her Georgia's face hadn't been tear-stained, nor bearing the tell-tale red puffiness that followed in the wake of one of her own crying jags. Despite her sharp temper the poor woman must have been holding back her grief-stricken tears in order to be brave for her little boy.

No wonder she'd erupted once help was at

hand. Seeing her little boy crawling amidst the unstable rubble, then hurting himself as he had, must have been terrifying. Especially in the wake of such a harrowing loss.

A small meow broke through the taut atmosphere.

Cailey froze, and felt Nicolas's mother go completely still too.

Theo took a step back from the exam table and gave Nicolas a sideways look. Stern, but not frightening. He clearly knew his way around children. What on earth had him so dead set against having his own? The man was a natural with them.

"Nicolas…" he began slowly. "Did you maybe bring a furry friend along to the clinic?"

Fear widened the little boy's eyes and he shot a panicked look toward his mother. Aware that everyone was looking at her, Georgia took a few tissues, blew her nose and tried to steady her breath. "Nicolas Georgiou Stephanopolous…"

"Meow!"

All eyes were drawn to the purple backpack Nicolas was carrying as something inside it began to wriggle frantically.

Cailey gave Georgia's hand a squeeze and took a step forward. "Nicolas, do you mind if we try and take your backpack off?"

The little boy shook his dark hair back and forth and then cried out in pain.

"Why don't we get that elbow back in place first?" Theo suggested, pulling out the last cactus barb. "Then we can take the backpack off and see who might be stowing away in it."

"I didn't put him in there," Nicolas blurted. "He crawled in when it was accidentally open."

The mewing grew in volume.

Georgia was the first to make a decision. She took two quick steps toward her son, unzipped the backpack and dipped her hands in. When she drew out the tiny ball of mewing fluff and turned it round to face her, everything in her softened.

"He has his eyes."

Theo sent her a questioning look.

"My Zeus. He had bright blue eyes like this."

She nuzzled the kitten, then pressed it to her cheek as once again tears cascaded from her eyes. A couple of moments passed and then she looked up at them all, ruffled an affectionate hand through her son's hair, dropped a kiss on the top of his head.

"You've done the right thing, love. You've done well." Choking on the next words she continued, "Your *baba* would be so proud."

Holding back tears of her own, Cailey helped Theo as he deftly saw to the dislocated elbow, explaining in his calm, steadying voice as they proceeded that Cailey was going to hold on to Nicolas as… One, two, three and *ooopa*! Look what they'd done. Put his elbow back in place!

"Now your funny bone will work again," Theo said moving his own arm back and forth.

"If I move my arm it will work now?"

Theo laughed. "Of course it will work. Give it a try."

"Right now?"

"If you're up to it."

Nicolas gave Theo a shocked expression which quickly turned to awe when he tried bending his arm and found it didn't hurt.

"Cailey, would you mind fitting Nicolas with one of our neoprene splints while I explain a few things to his mum about aftercare?"

Cailey shook her head, still as impressed as Nicolas was at how Theo had dealt with an intensely emotive situation.

"We'll just be out in the corridor when you're done." Theo bent down so he was eye to eye with Nicolas. "You look after Zeus, all right? But more importantly always, *always* listen to your mother. Especially now. The island is still healing. It's not made of strong muscles and bones like you."

Theo pointed out where the splinting supplies were to Cailey, then lowered his voice as

Georgia opened the door to the busy corridor. "I'm going to recommend she takes Nicolas out to the garden to play with his kitten and have a chat with Dr. Risi."

"The psychiatrist from Canada?"

"Greek-born, Canada-reared—yes. Lea specializes in trauma, and I think Georgia could probably do with a few coping skills…" He glanced across at Nicolas, who was staring glassy-eyed at the kitten nestling against his mother's chest. "The neoprene splint should do the trick. All right?"

She nodded, trying not to lean in and inhale him. This man had absolutely everything right…except the desire to commit.

Well…the desire to commit to *her*. And that was the nub of it.

She watched Theo leave the room, then turned on her brightest smile for Nicolas. "Let's get this splint on you—just for a bit of padding."

"I thought it was fixed?"

"It is, but sometimes things take a bit longer than we like to heal properly."

"Like Mummy's heart?"

"Exactly like Mummy's heart. And yours, too."

Cailey remembered her brothers, so brave after their father had died, stepping up without being asked. She couldn't remember either of them shedding a single tear.

After she'd eased on the neoprene splint and explained to Nicolas about giving his arm some rest, Cailey sat up on the exam table beside him.

"You want to look after Zeus, right?"

Nicolas nodded, his lips thinning in preparation for bad news.

"Sounds like a pretty good idea. Just make sure you save some extra care for your mummy too, all right?"

Unexpectedly Nicolas's face lit up from within. "She's the *best* mummy!"

"Good to hear." Cailey grinned, hopped down from the table, then lifted Nicolas down to the floor. "She is *definitely* raising a great little boy."

"Thank you, Cailey. I promise to be good."

Cailey got down on her knees, felt her heart aching for him and his mother as Nicolas threw his arms around her for a huge hug.

She took a deep breath of little-boy scent, vividly aware of how lucky Theo was to work at this island clinic. He'd get to see this little boy as he grew up. Perhaps the next time he saw him he'd be on the island's youth football team, then he'd have a girlfriend, maybe even get married himself one day and have a child of his own.

Her hand slipped to the soft curve of her belly. There wasn't a soul in London who would want the same for *her* child. If there was one, she firmly reminded herself.

She'd have to sneak a pregnancy kit out of the supplies cupboard when she had a moment.

A knock sounded on the door and Theo's face appeared while she was still hugging Nicolas.

"Apologies for interrupting!"

When Nicolas turned around, his face a huge grin, Theo smiled. Not the tear-fest he'd clearly been expecting.

"Ready to go out into the garden now?"

Nicolas nodded and ran to accept his mother's outstretched hand.

"Well done." Theo nodded toward the pair as they headed out to the courtyard garden, where Dr. Risi was holding informal talks with anyone who needed it.

She could probably do with a chat herself, Cailey thought wryly.

"You too," she said, realizing Theo was waiting for a response. "You're a good doctor."

"You're a good nurse."

She blushed. She knew she was good at her job. She'd almost literally worked her fingers to the bone to reach the top of her class. But hearing it from Theo, who'd actually become the doctor he'd vowed to be all those years ago, meant a lot.

"We could use someone like you around the clinic."

"I'm right here."

"But for how long?"

Good question. Nine months? Eighteen years? Forever?

She parted her lips to ask him if he had a few minutes to talk.

"Dr. Nikolaides?" A thirty-something doctor from Australia, whose family was originally from Greece, approached the pair of them.

Cailey had seen him coming in and out with the rescue crews working out of makeshift ambulances, but hadn't yet spoken with him.

"A bunch of us are going over to Stavros's *taverna* tonight. It'll be a good chance to wave off the crews heading back to the mainland in the morning. Fancy joining us?"

The Australian doctor looked at Cailey, did a quick double-take, then gave her a very slow, very obviously appreciative head-to-toe scan. "Well, g'day. *You're* most welcome to join us too, young lady. Dr. Alexis Giantopolous at your service—and you are…?"

"A very qualified, very respectable nurse,

born and bred right here on Mythelios, who doesn't take kindly to being patronized," Theo answered for her, through obviously clenched teeth.

Cailey's eyes popped wide open and she only just managed to stop her jaw from dropping. Was Theo *jealous*?

Theo slung a proprietorial arm over her shoulder. "We'll see how we go, Alexis. After the shift."

Cailey dropped her eyelids to half-mast and gave Theo a sidelong look. Two weeks of being pretty much ignored by him and all of a sudden they were a "we" when a bit of competition presented itself?

There had to be more to it than that. Nothing was that simple. If only she'd dreamt up an imaginary boyfriend or paid one of her study buddies to invite her to a dance in front of Theo all those years ago…

It still wouldn't have stopped his father from bullying her off the island.

And it still wouldn't make up for the fact that she'd completely forgotten to take the morning-after pill and could very well be carrying his baby.

"Right, then. I can see my extra-curricular talents will only go to waste here." Alexis took a very stagey step backwards and dropped a saucy wink in Cailey's direction. "Looks as though I need to find someone else to share this hot Australian bod with."

He stepped back again and "shot" them both with his index fingers.

"But you'll both be there, right? It's meant to be a ripper of a gathering!"

Cailey laughed and Theo grumbled.

"C'mon…" She gave him a little nudge and ducked out from under his arm. "It just might be fun."

CHAPTER TWELVE

"GIGANTES PLAKIS?"

Theo took the bean dish from Cailey and smiled. *"Efharisto.* Thank you."

"I still speak Greek, Theo. No need to translate."

Cailey took a long drink of water. There had been a bit of bite to her comment.

"Yes, of course. I know, it's just…" He sighed and scrubbed a hand across his face, feeling the fatigue as he spoke. "These long hours must be taking their toll."

"You've really worked hard."

He sought her face for any signs of derision. Animosity. There were none, but neither was there the usual light in her eyes, nor that ready laugh he'd heard brightening up the clinic when she worked with Dr. Balaban.

"You've worked hard, too. It's great to see you putting all your nursing training to use."

She shot him a look but said nothing.

"I mean, it's been nice to see you."

"Yes, well…next time there's an earthquake I'll be sure to come back and lend a hand."

"Do that, yes. Wait! You're not leaving, are you?"

"'Fraid so. I mean…unless you need me to stay. But things seem to be largely under control now."

"Yes, they are, but there's always room for a good nurse with excellent language skills."

Damn! He was being a complete and utter idiot! This was what he had in his casual banter arsenal? Platitudes that sounded as if they were straight out of a human resources manual?

Little wonder he was single. He had the panache of a sea slug. But couldn't she see he cared? That he was trying?

"Would you mind passing the salt, please?"

He handed it to her. "Local salt," he said. "Delicious."

She nodded her head as she took the salt shaker and began to put much more than any health professional would have ever recommended for daily consumption on her food.

Stop. Being. So. Thick.

She was trying to get his attention. Those angry shakes of the salt obviously had nothing to do with Stavros's ability to season calamari and a whole lot to do with the man sitting next to her.

A bolt of understanding hit him in the chest. Unless he stopped compartmentalizing he was never going to be able to give Cailey what she deserved. A peaceful resolution before she went back to London.

So it was either suck up the fact that she was going to leave this island with a subterranean opinion of him, or find some way to stick a crowbar in his heart and prove to her he cared.

Until now he'd only been thinking of things in black and white. He lived here. She lived in London. He couldn't do relationships.

But she didn't seem to *want* a relationship. Not anymore anyway.

It wasn't as if you gave her much of a chance, you idiot. Try again. Don't let her leave the island thinking you're a complete ass.

"Do you enjoy working with Dr. Balaban?"

"Yes."

Her answer was solid and genuinely positive. *Good.* Traction.

"I've really learned a lot from him."

"He's an excellent doctor."

"That he is."

"Enough to inspire you to try for med school?"

Her eyes did a few rapid blinks. He was losing ground. Touchy territory, from the looks of things.

"I think I'll stick with nursing, thanks."

"Good. Yes. You're great at nursing."

He was back-pedaling at a rate of knots but not entirely sure why. How did everything he said to her seem to morph into ramming each of his feet straight into his mouth?

Cailey nodded in acknowledgement, her eyes firmly glued on the plate of calamari working its way down the table.

Excellent. Not only had he clearly insulted her choice of career, but he was now officially less interesting than the island's most common food. Or, more to the point, less reliable.

He hadn't exactly made much time to speak with her over the past fortnight. If she were a patient he would have insisted on clearing the air. Making sure she understood.

His chest tightened as she stabbed a ring of calamari and squeezed juice from a wedge of lemon on to it.

He *had* made things clear to her. Crystal-clear. He didn't want a relationship. He didn't want a child. And he didn't bend those rules for anyone. But he'd just left her to take that wretched pill on her own and not given it one more moment's thought.

They were crowded onto a bench jammed

with people, but it felt as if the two of them were completely isolated. From the group. From each other.

He scanned the two long tables butted together in the courtyard area of the *taverna*, where the group had made a decision to eat family-style. Everyone seemed to be having a great time. Everyone but them.

When he looked back at Cailey her focus was still firmly on her plate.

"Everything okay?" He gave her a gentle nudge and a smile.

He knew he wasn't going to come out the good guy here, but he could do better than this. Cailey deserved more than a one-night stand and a cold shoulder when she had been nothing less than open and honest with him.

"Yup," she answered eventually, her voice tightly polite. "Stavros has outdone himself. Yum."

She pointed her fork at her plate and proceeded to rearrange her food. From what he'd seen she hadn't taken so much as a mouthful. Hardly the behavior of someone digging in and enjoying her meal.

He scanned the tables full of medical and rescue professionals, reliving their days, plucking stories from their pasts to dazzle one another with. Many of them had been to earthquakes before. Turkey. Tibet. One—the ever flirtatious Dr. Giantopolous—had even been to a quake in New Zealand. Everywhere the stories were the same. People coming together in times of adversity.

He could do it for his patients. He simply didn't have it in him to expose anyone to the insane dynamics of the Nikolaides family household.

The word "babies" started being bandied about regularly enough that he couldn't help but tune in.

"Elevator!" one of the ER techs shouted out.

"Been there, done that!" A redheaded nurse from Ireland pursed her lips. "Easy-peasy."

"Back of a taxi!" yelled another nurse.

"We've *all* done the back of a taxi," shot back Dr. Balaban from the far end of one of the tables.

"Twins? On your own? When it's you giving birth?" she challenged.

Dr. Balaban laughed, raised a glass and rose to make a bow of respect to her.

"I've helped deliver triplets." Another paramedic threw his hat into the ring.

"Quadruplets!" Cailey called.

Her eyes had become bright and her cheeks were pinkened up from the lively atmosphere. When the crowd cheered and pronounced her the winner they made her stand up and receive a full round of applause.

She was, Theo forced himself to acknowledge, the most beautiful woman in the room—both inside and out—and he was letting her just walk away from him.

Stavros arrived with a couple of flagons of red wine. Local, of course. He always championed the island's producers as much as he could.

When Theo began to dig into his pocket Stavros waved him off. "On the house," he said. "For everything you do."

He also received a rowdy round of applause and cheers.

Before he could leave, Theo stopped him. "How's the cut?"

"Good, good," the older man replied, his fingers lifting to the bandage on his head that looked freshly applied. "Cailey has been changing the plaster for me every day after her shift. The headaches come and go."

Theo's eyebrows knitted together. "What type of headaches?"

Stavros shrugged. "Don't you worry about it, young man. Bad in the morning...better by lunchtime. I'm fit as a fiddle right now." He tipped his head in Cailey's direction and lowered his voice. "You are looking after our Cailey *mou*?"

How on earth—?

Cool it. This was just one islander looking after another.

"Absolutely. She's doing an amazing job at the clinic."

"Yes." Stavros gave Theo a meaningful nod. "She is a true asset to the island."

Theo glanced at Cailey, her smile finally at full mast, engaged in a lively conversation with the Irish nurse across the table about the quadruplets.

"Yes, she is."

"Are you going to do anything about it?"

"Me?" Theo nearly choked on his wine. He had feelings for her, yes, but…

"Yes, you." Stavros looked at him quizzically. "Who else could offer her a job at the clinic?"

"Ah, yes. The clinic. Of course. Well, we are always happy to consider bringing local talent into the fold."

Stavros hadn't missed the *aha!* moment. A sly smile worked its way across his lips.

Theo opened his mouth to protest but Stavros waved it off. "No, no, my boy. None of my business. None of my business at all."

Theo knew as well as anyone born and bred

on Mythelios that "none of my business" meant that by morning the whole island would know Theo had set his hat at Cailey's door.

He turned back to the table of doctors, praying that he was about to become absorbed in a rigorous discussion about gall bladders.

"What about best excuses for surprise pregnancies?" a raucous EMT who was here on holiday from the States asked through a huge guffaw. "I bet I've heard 'em all."

The list swept from miracles to madness. Divine intervention took a lot of credit. As did numerous "secret tonics," blindfolds and sexy nurse costumes. All the nurses around the tables took a lot of ribbing at that one.

Cailey dipped her head, her expression hidden behind the spill of curls falling round her shoulders.

"Nobody's mentioned earthquakes," one doctor said when the table fell silent.

Everyone nodded for a moment, as if giving his statement its due weight—and then burst into hysterics.

"No, no. Seriously," the fifty-something doctor continued. "I've been to a lot of conflict zones, natural disasters—the lot. And without fail nine months later there's a rush in the maternity ward."

"What else are people going to do with no

television to distract them?" Alexis asked. "Rhetorical question, obviously."

He scanned the table until he caught Cailey's eye and dropped her a slow, meaningful wink.

Theo swallowed hard. He told himself he wasn't about to punch the guy…but his fingers had curled instinctively into fists.

"Well," cut in a seasoned nurse from Athens, "an earthquake is a *much* better excuse than faulty protection or forgetting to take the morning-after pill! I mean, *seriously*! Who has ever met someone who has *genuinely* forgotten to take the morning-after pill?"

Theo forced himself to chuckle along. It had been a far from ideal solution, but at least he and Cailey had managed to cover their bases after their own "accident."

Instinctively, he turned to Cailey.

All the color had drained from her face.

And as he registered what her ashen complexion implied he felt the blood drain from his own.

Cailey couldn't get out of the *taverna* fast enough.

The look of horror on Theo's face had told her everything she needed to know.

She'd made the biggest mistake of her life.

Her feet picked up the pace and before she

knew what was happening she was running down the main street toward the beach, as if there wasn't enough air in the busy thoroughfare to fill her lungs.

When she'd taken the pregnancy test after her shift all she'd wanted to do was go home. Then Theo had stopped her in the hallway and all but insisted she come along to the *taverna*.

Trust him to want to keep up appearances when curling up in a ball on her mother's sofa was what she would rather be doing. It was the Nikolaides way, it seemed. Showing one face to the world and hiding the real one in the shadows.

But really? This time she was no different.

She was carrying his child after having pretty much agreed to take the morning-after pill.

It had been an honest mistake, but it was one Theo would very likely never forgive her for.

She ran and ran until she reached the beach, where she kicked off her trainers, tied up the skirt she'd pulled on after changing out of her scrubs and waded straight into the sea.

As the surf hit her feet and then her shins she forced herself to time her breathing with the cadence of the waves. In and out. In and out. Hyperventilating and fainting into a high tide wasn't going to help anything. Not with a baby growing inside her.

She offered the ocean a grim smile. See? Proof positive that she could still be practical about *some* things.

Too bad she hadn't been so sensible with her heart.

When she'd seen those two pink lines appear on the pregnancy test her heart had flipped... with *joy*.

She loved Theo. She always had. Yes, he was flawed. But who wasn't? She had a Mythelios-sized chip on her own shoulder because she'd never be a doctor. Surely Theo was allowed foibles of his own.

Did it break her heart that he didn't love her back? More than she would probably ever admit. But when it came down to it every cell in her body was over the moon that she hadn't taken that pill. She *wanted* this baby. *His* baby. And she would do everything in her power to make sure it was healthy and happy.

As if on cue a full moon came out from beneath a pile of clouds, its powerful light hitting the sea like a fistful of silver glitter. An endorsement from the heavens if ever there was one. Her hands folded protectively over her stomach. Her first proper maternal instinct.

Made to assure the life growing inside her that she would do everything she could to protect it.

Right. If she was mature enough to have a child on her own, she had to be mature enough to talk to Theo and confirm his suspicions. He had a right to know for definite that he was going to become a father, whether he liked it or not. And she had a lot of thinking to do.

She turned around and made her way up to the beach, grabbed her shoes and headed back toward the clinic.

No point in delaying the inevitable.

She needed to start putting her exit plan into place as soon as possible.

"Dr. Nikolaides!"

Lea Risi was running out of the clinic, waving her arms at him. Agitation coursed through him. Couldn't she see he was busy?

"It's Georgia Stephanopolous. There aren't any doctors at the clinic and she's gone into early labor!"

Theo did an abrupt about-face. He was about to say, *You're a doctor—you fix it.* But Lea had made it clear that psychiatry was her specialty, and she had already been unbelievably generous with her time and skills. He had no doubt she would have seen Georgia through the birth if she could. But a truly talented doctor knew when to ask for help—and Dr. Risi was one of the best.

He shot a look down the darkened street. No sign of Cailey. Whether she had fled the *taverna* out of guilt or fear was beyond him, but it hurt him to the quick that she had run away from him.

"How early is she?"

"Four weeks."

Dammit.

However much he wanted to get to Cailey, talk to her about what was going on, he couldn't leave a patient.

Thirty-six weeks wasn't so early that the baby's health would be dramatically compromised, but it was still moderately premature. A mental list of possible issues started to fall into place. Low birth weight. Blood sugar. Breathing problems. Jaundice. Trouble latching on and feeding.

And on it went. There were enough variables that he needed to be there.

"Right." He knew he looked as grim as he sounded. "Let's go."

When they reached the clinic Lea pointed him toward the makeshift resus area, where he could hear a nurse encouraging Georgia to breathe through the contractions.

"I've put her in here. It seemed to have the most equipment in case—" She stopped, unable to put words to the unthinkable. *In case it all went wrong.* "I'm really sorry, Dr. Nikolaides. I know you've hardly had an hour outside of the clinic, but…"

"Don't worry. Honestly. And thank you." He gave her arm a quick squeeze. "You've done the right thing. Upstairs there's a room with a neonatal cot in it. Would you mind bringing that down?"

She shot an anxious glance toward the courtyard garden. "I've left Nicolas on his own… well, with his kitten…in the garden. We were all having a bit of a play together when the first contractions hit."

His phone rang. He swore under his breath. Didn't he have enough on his plate? He pulled the phone out of his pocket.

Cailey. The last person he'd expected to be on the other end of the line.

He showed the phone to Lea. "Cailey Tomaras. She's a neonatal nurse."

And she was very likely pregnant with his child.

He took the call. "Cailey?"

"We need to talk."

"Absolutely. We do. I'm just at the clinic. Georgia Stephanopolous is in labor."

"But that's too early!"

The instant concern in her voice told him all he needed to know. She would come if he asked.

Get over yourself, your issues with your father, and ask her to help you. The best doctors know when to ask for help.

"Can you come straight here?"

"Of course."

Relief flooded through him. He'd delivered babies before, even preemies, but never when he was wondering about the welfare of the mother of his *own* child.

"I'll just go and get Nicolas, shall I?" Lea was already heading out to the garden. "I'll ask Cailey to fetch down the cot when she gets here."

"Good—fine. Thank you!"

He popped into the screened-off area where Georgia was pacing from window to exam table and back again like a caged tiger. When she turned to face him her expression was frantic with fear.

"He should be here!"

He knew who she meant. Her husband. The man who had fathered her child and who had been so cruelly taken from her. No doubt the trauma of losing him so tragically had brought on her labor early.

And you should be there for Cailey.

Unable to find the best way to answer, he gave her a nod. "You just keep telling us everything you're experiencing and we'll do the best we can for you and your baby. I'll go and scrub up and be back with you in a minute." He looked at the nurse who was busy setting up the monitors. "Cassandra, do you have everything you need?"

"Everything but the cot," she said evenly.

Cassandra was in her early fifties. She'd had four children of her own, so this was familiar territory for her.

"Georgia's not too far from the active phase, so you go on and scrub up. We'll be just fine."

He gave her a nod of thanks and headed to the supplies cupboard to get a surgical gown to cover his street clothes.

Out of the corner of his eye Theo saw a familiar tangle of dark curls working its way through the smattering of people still seeking refuge in the clinic's large foyer.

His heart leapt and crashed against his ribcage.

"Cailey!"

She turned at the sound of her name and quickly picked up her pace. In the opposite direction.

He jogged through the triage area and caught up to her, grabbing one of her hands.

She yanked it away as if she'd been branded.

There were countless things he should be saying to her. *Are you really carrying my child? What can I do to help? Can you believe me when I say that I care for you but that I am not the man you deserve?*

Instead he pulled a surgical gown out of a nearby cupboard and asked, "Are you happy to scrub in?"

A glaze of tears sprang to her eyes but her voice was cool. "Of course. Dr. Risi has asked me to get the cot from upstairs, which is where I'm headed, and then I'll be right down."

A sharp, intense battle lit up his heart. Was he going to choose his father's path of ignoring anything emotional? Anything painful? Or was it time to man up and face reality—no matter how painful?

He reached out and took hold of her hand again, held it firmly. "Are you carrying my child?"

"*Our* child," she retorted, fireworks flaring in her eyes in a series of bright sparks. "*Our* child."

She leant in close, so that a passing nurse wouldn't overhear her.

"And before you have a chance to launch into

any recriminations—yes. I was an idiot. Yes. I forgot to take that wretched pill. Do I regret it?" She didn't wait for him to answer. "*Not. For. A. Second.* But don't worry. I won't be trying to get anything from you. So let's just make this simple, shall we? From now on we'll call this baby *mine.*"

He was so much caught by surprise at her fierce claim on the child he released her hand.

She massaged her wrist with her other hand and eyed him almost clinically. For someone who had gazed at him before with something little short of love—

Christos.

She *loved* him.

Which made admitting he didn't believe he was capable of the depth of love she deserved all the more painful.

"Dr. Nikolaides?"

Cassandra was calling from down the hall and beckoning to him.

"On my way."

He looked Cailey straight in the eye. One way or the other he'd do right by her.

"This isn't finished. We'll talk about it later."

"Fine." She gave him a curt nod and headed off to the lifts.

CHAPTER THIRTEEN

"YOU CAN DO THIS, Georgia." Cailey pressed a cold cloth to her forehead and gave her hand a squeeze.

"I don't want it to come out yet! I'm not ready!"

"Of course you are."

"No!" Tears streamed down Georgia's face as she fought the intensity of another contraction. "I can't bear that my husband won't ever see him!"

"Her blood pressure is increasing." Theo's voice was calm. Steady.

Cailey nodded her acknowledgement. She knew what he was saying. Georgia's emotions were getting the better of her, and any distress the mother was feeling would transfer straight to the baby.

"We're here for you, Georgia," Theo said. "You have everything you need right here."

If only "Dr. Theo" was on a par with "real-life Theo," thought Cailey Then she wouldn't feel she had to shoulder the guilt for getting pregnant.

Give yourself a break. It was an honest mistake. And you're going to deal with it. On your own.

Cailey gave Georgia's forehead another wipe and smiled at her. Her heart ached for the woman. Widowed so young. A little boy to look after. No income now that her husband was gone. A baby about to come into the world and yet…

"I've got an idea." She positioned herself so Georgia could see her face. "What do you say we get Nicolas in here to hold your hand? Dr. Risi can come, too."

Georgia shook her head back and forth. "Not like this. I don't want him to see me like this."

"Your little boy is made of courage. He wants to help you."

"But it's my job to look after *him*," Georgia sobbed. "How can I do that now that my husband is gone?"

"You can and you will," Cailey said with conviction. "I've seen how you two are together." She softened her voice. "Let your son help you through this. He wants to help."

Despite her vow not to look at Theo, her eyes crept toward him. Above his face mask she met his unwavering gaze. She was almost shocked when he didn't look away.

Was that what he'd been trying to say out in the corridor earlier? That help might not be coming in the way she wanted it to but he would try?

"Get him. Get my boy."

Cailey nodded and handed the cloth to Cassandra. "Back in a minute."

A few minutes later Nicolas had his mother in stitches as he mimicked her howls of pain.

"You sound like a werewolf," she gasped as another contraction hit.

"You *do*, Mama!" His eyes widened. "Ooh. That one sounds the worst."

"It's the most powerful so far," Theo said, his eyes focused beneath the blue drape over Georgia's knees. "Cailey, can you come here for a minute?"

"Absolutely."

"Georgia, we need you to give another big push."

Just as Cailey reached Theo's side the head emerged. Cailey deftly suctioned the mouth and nose.

"Just one more push now…and it looks like you have become a big brother, Nicolas. Well done!"

"Boy or girl?" Georgia asked, wilting back

against the pillows with equal parts relief and exhaustion.

Theo nodded at Cailey to hold the newly delivered baby while he made swift work of clamping the umbilical cord.

"You have just had a beautiful little girl."

Cailey didn't look at him, but she could have sworn his voice had cracked as he'd delivered the news.

She swiftly wiped the baby clean. "We're just going to dry her off, to help keep her warm."

"Why does she need to be warm? It's almost summer outside," Nicolas asked.

"Little babies can't control their temperatures as well as you can, so it's important for her to be warm and right here on your mummy's chest."

Cailey lowered the baby into Georgia's arms relishing the moment. This was one of her favorite parts of being a neonatal nurse.

"Cailey?" Theo's voice was questioning.

She bristled. She knew what he was asking. Why haven't you suctioned her again? Why haven't you swaddled her yet? Or taken the blood tests? Or done the thousand other things neonatal nurses were meant to do?

She could feel Cassandra staring at her. Waiting for her to take the lead. This was, after all, her specialty.

And then it hit her. This *was* her area of expertise. Her mother was right. She loved her job. Loved what she did. Being a doctor had been a dream, but so had being a princess and if the gossip magazines were anything to go by being a princess wasn't all it was cracked up to be.

"I tend to let new mums have a moment with the baby before all the tests begin," Cailey explained. "And leaving the umbilical cord for a few minutes gives extra blood-flow, which should help reduce the chances of anemia and iron deficiency."

She noticed Nicolas reaching out toward his little sister and then pulling his hand back when he saw her watching him.

"Go on. It's all right to touch her."

Everyone stopped and watched as Nicolas reached out his small hand toward his sister's even tinier one. When their fingers touched the baby blinked, her blue eyes connecting first with Nicolas and then Georgia before closing again.

Cailey's heart squeezed tight and then all but exploded. This was what it was all about. Pure, organic love.

She glanced at Theo, who was preparing to deliver the placenta. "Are you happy for me to do the Apgar assessment?"

Theo nodded. Was his lack of verbal response an emotional reaction to the birth? Or just further proof that he didn't want children of his own?

Heaven knew she was feeling all sorts of emotions. Joy, relief, fear, excitement. And that was just for Georgia! If she was going to do her job properly she couldn't even *begin* to address what she was feeling. She looked across to Cassandra and smiled. The seasoned nurse wasn't even bothering to wipe away the tears freely rolling down her cheeks.

"She is an absolute beauty."

"I'm really sorry to have to do this." Cailey reached out and took the little girl. "We just need to run a few tests."

"Why? Is something wrong? Is this because she was born early?" Georgia pushed herself up and reached out for her child—her mother's instinct to protect at its highest level.

"She looks fine to me," Cailey soothed. "She's pinking up nicely. If you remember when Nicolas was born, the medical staff would've done all of the same tests."

"I was born in a boat!" Nicolas beamed.

Georgia gave a light laugh and fell back to her pillows. "Nicolas's father thought he would help me go into labor by rowing me around in a boat. It turned out to be too good a tactic.

Nicolas was born about one hundred meters from the shore."

"Sounds like quite a surprise," Cailey said as she began quickly checking the baby's heart-rate and taking notes on her breathing, muscle tone, and gently turning her head to the side to check her asymmetrical tonic neck reflex. Her right arm flexed and the left arm reached out from the body as her tiny fingers began to uncurl. Perfect.

"It *was* a surprise," Georgia said, pulling her son to her for a hug. "*He* was a surprise."

"Oh?" Cassandra asked.

"Let's just say my husband and I hadn't exactly planned on being parents so soon."

"Ah, well…" Cassandra laughed. "It happens to the best of us." She smiled at Georgia, then looked to Theo and Cailey for their smiles only to find none.

"Hmm." Cassandra sniffed as she shrugged off the lack of response from her colleagues. "I guess it's just you and me, then."

About an hour later, after the placenta had been safely delivered and Cailey had finished the rest of her tests and put the baby in the warm neo-natal cot as Georgia snuggled up with Nicolas for some sleep, their work was done. Cassan-

dra had to head home so Cailey volunteered to
stay with Juno, the newborn little girl, until the
morning shift arrived.

Sitting quietly with the infant—small at two
and a half kilos, but in perfect health otherwise—was every bit the tonic it had been at
the hospital in England.

She was so absorbed in watching the little
girl's fingers as they twitched and curled in her
sleep that she hardly noticed Theo walking in.

"Everything all right?"

Something about his demeanor said he
needed to be here as much as she did. She
pulled a chair up alongside the incubator and
patted it.

"I owe you an apology—" she began. He
made a move as if to interrupt, but she held
up a hand to stop him. "Sit. Relax. And before
you ask—which is your right—I didn't do it
on purpose."

His eyes were on Juno, just as hers were, but
she was sure he could feel the energy buzzing
between the pair of them.

"I never thought that, Cailey. Not for one
second. But you know how I feel about becoming a father."

"I know, and I'm so sorry, but…" She'd
wanted to scream and yell, but just as quickly

the urge left her. She squeezed her eyes tight and drew in a breath. Shouting at him wasn't going to change anything, let alone help the situation. "I'm sorry. It was a genuine oversight."

"Wasn't the pill in your pocket?"

"It was," she conceded. "It must've fallen out when I took my clothes off, or got tangled with a tissue or something. Whatever it was… things were so busy, and I guess it was out of sight, out of mind because—"

"Life took over," he finished for her, nodding along, as if the same thing might have happened to him, given how chaotic things had been over the past fortnight.

It had really only been in the last day or so that life at the clinic had begun to feel less like a crisis and more like a recovery.

Cailey put her hand on the clear dome of Juno's crib and spread her fingers wide, then yawned.

"Do you want me to stay?"

"No, no. I'll be all right. I texted Mum and she said she'd bring over some coffee and baklava in a bit."

"She's a good woman," Theo said.

"She's a good *mother*," Cailey countered, and instantly regretted the clarification. It wasn't like she was trying to rub it in. She was just shoring up all the time with her mother that she could before she went back to her life in London.

"And you will be too."

She turned and looked at him, but said nothing. She wished it didn't hurt so much that Theo's voice was tinged with sadness. Sorrowful or not, it was the words he *didn't* say that sat between them like an untethered lion.

She forced herself to put a voice to the thoughts they were both thinking. "I'm guessing you don't want to be involved at all."

He looked at her for a moment, his cheeks hollowing as he considered what to say. In the end he shook his head. "But I won't leave you to pay for everything on your own, obviously."

"Obviously," she repeated with more than a hint of acerbity. "After all, it's the Nikolaides way, isn't it?"

Theo's forehead instantly crinkled into deep furrows.

She held up a hand. "Please. Don't bother. I don't want your money. I never wanted anything from you. Not a free pass to medical school. Not a leg up on the society pages. No matter what your father told you, I never took so much as a cent from him. When he ordered me to leave Mythelios ten years ago I did as I was told. Just like a good little servant girl.

Don't worry. I'll do it again. Only this time I'm going to do it with my head held high."

He shot her a look of disbelief and something deep within her bridled.

"What? A person can't just love another person for themselves?" She didn't give him a chance to answer when she saw him raise his eyebrows in surprise. "As if you didn't know. C'mon, Theo. I know you weren't born yesterday. I thought leaving Mythelios would be enough to cure me of you, but then I was stupid enough to open my heart to you a second time. But now that I know you're just like your father—solving all your problems with money—I'm pretty sure I'll be able to get over it. Over *you*."

His lack of response was like swallowing broken glass.

So. That was that. She was going to be raising a child on her own.

Was it in the circumstances she'd thought? Not at all. But she'd do everything in her power to give this baby the best life possible.

She was going to have to take a leaf out of the Mythelios islanders' book and rise above it, even if her heart was breaking.

It would mend.

Mostly.

"Well, then." She crossed her arms over her

chest and leaned back in her chair. "If you don't mind, I guess it's time I heard why you did what you did ten years ago."

CHAPTER FOURTEEN

THEO STARED AT HER, his heart pounding against his ribcage in double-time.

His father had tried to *pay* her to leave? The sheer audacity of it all but blindsided him. Pieces in the jigsaw puzzle he'd never known he was putting together began to fall into place.

Erianthe's departure… He'd been told she needed better schooling, but afterwards she'd never been the same, carefree, fun-loving wild child that she'd been before then.

And Cailey's departure had been fairly sharpish after Erianthe's.

Her mother had said it was to do with nursing college and he hadn't even thought to question it. People chose paths and followed them. Just as he'd followed his own. And in so doing he had clearly been completely oblivious to everything happening around him.

"I never asked my father to talk to you."

"Yeah, *right*." She actually laughed.

Cailey deserved the truth, so he sucked in a sharp breath, looked her straight in the eye and said, "I'm not my father's son."

Cailey drew back in surprise. "I'm sorry?"

"I'm adopted," he clarified, before realizing that the look on Cailey's face was more relieved than horrified.

It had never occurred to him that people might see it as a *good* thing.

"So…what exactly are you saying? I'm supposed to feel sorry for you for being adopted by a billionaire and given all of the opportunities in the world?"

"Hardly. Pity is the last thing I deserve. Or want. You're right in some ways, but not in others. I hit the jackpot. I had everything I wanted as I grew up…everything but love."

Cailey sucked in a breath, no doubt about to say something along the lines of *Boo-hoo, you poor little rich kid.*

He held up a hand, vividly aware of the small baby lying in the incubator right in front of him.

He could have this if he wanted. A child. A woman who loved him… Though he had a lot of apologizing to do if he was ever going to get her to trust him again.

Just tell her the truth! Tell her what you feel.

"I lack the power to connect. With anyone."

"What?" Her nose crinkled as she looked at him in disbelief. "That's utterly ridiculous. You're amazing with your patients. And you and Erianthe were always close."

He tipped his head back and forth. "Until she went away, yes. Afterwards—not so much."

"So why didn't you stay in closer contact?"

"That's not what Nikolaides *do*!"

He stopped himself short of slamming his hand down on the counter running alongside him. He was raging against the wrong person. Taking it out on the one woman who deserved to be treated with kid glove tenderness. But he'd never voiced any of this before, fearing the thoughts he'd long suppressed would do one thing and one thing only: manifest themselves as rage. The one emotion that came so easily to the Nikolaides household.

Determination obviously flourished in the Tomaras family, because Cailey was still sitting there. Waiting. She wasn't going to let him off the hook. Not easily.

The silence between them hummed with tension.

He felt fearless when it came to medicine. And utterly defenseless in the face of becoming a father. It was a responsibility he was simply incapable of fulfilling.

History had taught him that.

Protecting Erianthe and his mother from his father's rages had been the only thing stopping him from running away as a boy. But his instinct had been to run. Not to stay.

And the only reason he stayed now was a little boy's pitiful need for his father's love. A love he would never receive. A love he would never be able to give to his own child.

Cailey stared at him, her dark eyes unwavering. In a completely dispassionate voice he'd never heard from her before she asked, "So what is it the Nikolaides 'do'?"

"What do you mean?"

Her upper lip twitched, as if she was resisting the temptation to sneer. "I'm already very aware of what they *don't* do. Marrying housemaids, for example."

"What do you mean?" He felt as if he'd been slammed against a wall.

"That little gem came straight from the horse's mouth," she said almost casually, as if telling him the island was due for yet another sunny day.

He huffed out a hollow laugh. "If that's something my father said, I wouldn't be surprised."

"Actually, your father said a lot of things. He said I wasn't worthy of you. He said I'd be nothing more than a housemaid. He said he'd make sure I never so much as put a toe inside any hospital you worked in so long as he drew breath. He was willing to pay me, of course. To protect you from my evil clutches."

"What are you talking about?" Theo could barely hear above the roar of fury raging in his head. He'd never heard any of this.

"Didn't he tell you?" Cailey asked, as if they were discussing the days of the week milk was delivered. "He told me if I didn't leave his house, leave Erianthe to her studies and, more to the point, leave you alone he would make sure my mother, my brothers and me never found work on this island again."

"But we weren't together."

"No. But he must've sensed there was something between us. Chemistry. The possibility of something developing."

"And then he told you a Nikolaides would never marry a housemaid?" Theo could hardly believe he was hearing this.

"Not exactly." She spread out her hand in front of her and looked at her fingernails. Her expression was maddeningly indecipherable when she eventually looked up at him. "You said it."

Frustration crashed through his intentions to do this rationally, calmly. Proof—as if he needed more—that he was right to step away now. He *never* would have said such a thing to

Cailey. His mind reeled back through memory after memory, trying to find the moment—*any* moment—when he would have said something so reprehensible and came up blank.

"No. Sorry, Cailey. You know me better than that. I would never have said something like that."

Cailey shook her head sadly, as if trying to reason with an unruly child. "I'm afraid I heard you say it to your friends."

"Not a chance. I don't feel that way. Only pure luck meant I didn't grow up in an orphanage. My father reminded me of that again and again, just as he—"

Ah. His father. Of course. Where else would such a hateful, divisive thought come from?

It all came back to him now. His father had just sent Erianthe off to boarding school and Theo had been putting his foot down over his plans to be a GP rather than some globally lauded heart surgeon.

His father had been railing at him about not wanting to throw good money after such pathetic goals. He wasn't paying for Theo to waste away his life in a backwater clinic and marry a housekeeper, he'd shouted. He wasn't paying for Theo to be common. Not on *his* watch. Not with *his* money.

It had been the precursor to their final stand-off. Though he thought he'd won at the time, he could see now that his father had been the victor after all.

Sure, Theo had become a GP. But at a cost…

He'd never have a family of his own. Never love and live with any sort of freedom of the heart.

The bitterness he'd always directed at his father threatened to consume him. He'd worked so hard to be a better man. A kinder man. But one look into Cailey's disappointed face told him his worst nightmare had in fact come true. He'd become exactly what his father had hoped for. A cool, distant, impartial bastard.

A thick, steel rod of pain shunted through him as he accepted the mantle. It was the only way he could get Cailey to see he should never parent a child.

"You asked what us Nikolaides do instead of caring?"

She nodded, blinking against the obvious threat of tears. He swallowed down an urge to console her, pull her into his arms and try to wash away the cruel words he'd already burdened her with. Instead he ploughed ahead— just as his father would have done.

"They work. They create fiefdoms where they can wield power. They're better off living alone."

Cailey blinked again and swiped at her eyes, absorbing his blunt assessment of his own family. "I see."

The coolness in her voice wrapped round his heart and twisted it with sharp, unrelenting force.

"Well, then." She pushed up from her chair and looked up at him. "If you don't mind, I'd like to watch Juno on my own tonight. In the morning I'll be gone."

He nodded. He understood. "That's fine. We've got enough staff to cover the clinic now."

She winced and he didn't blame her. She was the mother of his child and all he was concerned about were staff rotas.

It might be painful as hell, but all of this was for the best.

"And don't…" she cautioned as he turned to leave. "Don't you ever try to get in touch with me or my child once I'm gone. Understood?"

He neither nodded nor protested. In the long run she'd see he was right to do this.

The moment he'd left the room, the depth of his loss hit him with Mach force strength. After a quick check on Georgia and Nicolas he walked out to the pier and stared out into the black night.

Knowing he would never have Cailey in his life felt akin to someone reaching into his chest and pulling his heart out of his ribcage. Without his having even noticed it, she had *become* his heart.

How could he not have seen it?

When she smiled, his world was brighter.

When she laughed, people glowed. *He* glowed.

She was passionate. Committed. Loving. Warm. Generous-hearted. Everything he could ever imagine wanting in a woman. A wife.

Cailey Tomaras. The one woman he had never let himself truly love. And yet here it was…love. Standing up proud like a soldier prepared to go into battle to fight for what it most valued, what was most vital in his life.

He loved Cailey.

Yes, they had shared one perfect night together, but in reality it could have been a million. That was how deeply she was embedded in his heart.

He couldn't believe he'd been so blind to the role she'd played in his life. They'd known each since they were children. Played together. Scraped knees together. He knew what made her laugh. What songs made her jump up and dance. That even the slightest bit of a breeze would untether one of her curls and let it frolic in the wind. And yet…

He hadn't remembered she'd always wished to be a doctor. It hadn't even occurred to him that her career as a nurse might feel like second-best to her. How could you know so much about one person, ache to know so much more, and still let them go?

The day Erianthe had been sent away sprang to mind. Cailey had come over, mystified that her best friend had left without so much as a goodbye. He'd had nothing to offer by way of an explanation. Dimitri had his ways, he'd said. He'd done his best to be a shoulder to cry on. She'd thrown her arms around his neck after he'd dried her tears and he'd wanted nothing more than to kiss her again, like he'd done that one time by the pool, but he hadn't.

Two days later she'd left and he'd never seen her again until recently.

He could blame Dimitri all he liked, but he'd let her slip through his fingers then and now the full depth of his love was being slashed in two as reality slammed into him.

Once again he was letting her go.

For a good reason, he reminded himself.

Their child would live a happy life. Cailey had enough love in her heart for the two of them. Her family would no doubt close ranks around her with the fathomless love and support he'd seen them offer one another through the years.

Any salve to his conscience evaporated.

And he would be no better than the parents who had abandoned him. He was choosing the coward's way out.

He would never forgive himself for it, but he would pray that one day Cailey would understand that he had done what was best for all of them.

Cailey stared out the window of the hospital staffroom, vividly aware that the dull, lackluster British summer sky mirrored her own mood.

Listless was a better word.

Ever since she'd returned to London a fortnight ago her entire body had felt out of sync… as if she'd gone through a time warp in Greece and was unable to get herself back to reality. Back to the life she had vowed to lead.

"Everything all right, Cailey?"

One of her favorite colleagues, Elise, handed her a cup of tea with a grin.

"Minty tea with a drop of honey. I don't know how you do these long days without caffeine." She raised her own glass of tar-thick coffee and gave a sheepish grin. "It's like I tell all my patients. Do as I say, not as I do."

Cailey smiled and accepted the warm mug. "Thank you, Elise. It smells great."

"It must've been tough."

"What?" Cailey hadn't said a word about Theo or the baby. How did Elise know?

"Working there after the earthquake. I've never done anything like that. You're very brave, Cailey."

And very stupid, she thought, willing herself to squash the image of Theo that inevitably popped into her mind only about a hundred thousand times a day.

"Well, cheers to you, love. May we all learn from you and your incredible strength."

They each took a thoughtful sip of their drinks.

"Biscuit for your thoughts?"

Elise jiggled a biscuit tin in front of Cailey. She shook her head. She hadn't been all that hungry lately. She took her vitamins, but each time she prepared a meal and sat down to eat it her hunger just vanished.

"Go on. I've not seen you eat a proper meal since you came back."

Cailey took a biscuit and made a show of enjoying a small nibble.

Elise beamed and gave her back a rub, instinctively sensing her friend's need for a bit of comfort.

"It'll be all right, love. I'm sure everyone back home was ever so grateful for all of the work you did over there."

Everyone but the one who counted most.

"Right." Elise tucked a couple more biscuits into Cailey's front pocket and gave her cheek a friendly peck. "I've got to get back on the ward. Take as long as you need."

As Elise disappeared out to the busy ward Cailey reminded herself these were the moments she needed to latch on to. Small, to be sure, but even the tiniest of reminders that she was building a life here in the UK was a positive step forward.

After she'd made it more than clear that her intention was to stay in London—no matter how much she longed to be with her family— her mother had promised to come over when the baby was born. A smile crept to her lips. As if she'd be able to keep the headstrong *yiayia* away.

Her brothers had been equally inflexible about their travel plans. And her sisters-in-law. They'd all piled on their promises of help, refusing to listen to her protestations that she'd be fine. Building cradles, changing tables. Knitting caps, jumpers—whatever she required. They'd promised her everything she needed, but they were unable to deliver on the one thing she wanted.

Theo.

None of them had pressed. None had pushed.

There was no need for them to ask questions about the father, she'd realized. Her heartbreak had been written all over her face.

She reached up to touch the necklace her mother had pressed into her hand when they'd walked to the ferry dock together. Her finger traced the tiny gold phoenix. It was a gift her father had given her mother to wear when he was out at sea.

"Put this on, love," her mother had said, tears sparkling in her eyes. "I know you think things are impossible now, but…like me…you will rise like the beautiful phoenix who lives in here."

Her mother had put her hand above Cailey's heart, then pulled her daughter to her for a deep, strong hug, as if trying her best to transfer the strength she'd gained from surmounting life's deepest sorrows.

If her mother could raise three young children on her own and stay as positive and loving as she had, then so could she. She was a Tomaras! And she would do what Tomarases had done from the beginning of time: rise from the ashes life had thrown in their path and fly.

"Are you ready to bring another baby into the world?"

Elise's voice jolted Cailey back into the present.

The question was far more pointed than Elise could ever know.

Her hand shifted to the tiny life only just gaining a foothold.

"Yes." She nodded, feeling something shift inside her, as if the first flutterings of the phoenix were those of the very child she was carrying in her womb. "Yes, I am."

CHAPTER FIFTEEN

THEO LOOKED UP from the stack of paperwork he'd been trying to plow his way through when the singing began.

What the…?

How had the entire staff managed to circle around him at the reception desk without his even having noticed?

Instead of "Happy Birthday" they were singing "Happy Anniversary."

Petra was standing in the center of the staff members, now whittled down to the people who regularly worked at the clinic as the need for clinicians from the mainland had abated.

As their song peaked he finally registered what they were singing for.

The clinic.

The four candles atop the ridiculously enormous cake Petra was sagging under were for each year the clinic had been up and running.

He should feel pride.

He should feel happy.

All he felt was a bone-aching sorrow that the woman who should be by his side was gone.

Petra, who seemed to know everything without having it spelled out for her, saw his expression shift from confusion to understanding to pain.

She hoisted the large cake onto the counter. "Make a wish," she commanded.

He opened his mouth to protest, only to have her cluck away his attempt to kick up a fuss.

Petra, like Cailey's mother, knew how to keep Theo in line.

The thought brought a smile to his face.

He could see Cailey doing the same. Reprimanding a toddler for wanting more cake or ice cream before gathering it in her arms and giving it a huge kiss. It was the Greek mother's way. Firm but unconditional love.

"Go on." Petra nudged the cake across the high counter. "Wish."

He scanned the smiling faces of the people who had helped bring this clinic to life.

The doctors, nurses, technicians…everyone who had stepped through the clinic doors…all of them had not only offered their services to improve the welfare of their fellow islanders, but had done so from their hearts.

His eyes flicked to the calendar hanging over

the reception desk, no longer turned to "his" month, but flicked over to Cailey's brother Kyros now, posing in his firefighter's uniform. Next month was Deakin's photo. He'd be arriving soon, from whichever African nation he'd been traveling in most recently. Then Ares. Then Chris. As they'd promised. In their own ramshackle way they would all manage to be there. Lend a hand when he needed it most.

Not a single one of them shared his blood, and yet...they were his brothers.

He lifted his gaze from the cake and stared at the staff in wonder—as if seeing them for the very first time. These people believed in him. They had all forsaken high-paying jobs on the mainland to help him bring quality medical care to the islanders. Without question, they had invested their futures in him, believing him to be dependable, kind, a man of moral integrity. A leader.

And he *was* those things. For the staff. For his patients.

But not for Cailey. And not for his father.

Today was the day that would change.

Every face looking so expectantly upon him now deserved for him to be the man they already believed him to be.

Having a child wasn't a problem. It was an opportunity. A chance to prove again and again that he had it in him to become the man he had always wanted to be.

He smiled at his team, and then at the flickering candles. He knew what he was going to wish for. And he knew what he would spend each and every moment of the rest of his life trying to do.

"Thank you," he said, feeling more indebted to the clinic staff than he could ever express. "If anything, I owe a debt of thanks to each and every one of you. Without your help—your tenacity and your faith—we wouldn't have made it through the first day the clinic doors opened, let alone been able to help the people of Mythelios when the earthquake hit. You have all helped to make this clinic the success story it is and will continue to be."

He looked down at the candles, then up at Petra. "It may have taken me a while to catch on, but I think you know what I am going to wish for."

She nodded.

Of course she did.

Petra knew everything.

"In which case..." Theo's lips parted in the first genuine smile he'd given in the weeks since Cailey had left Mythelios "...let's all make sure this works."

He gestured for everyone to gather in close

and—as with most things in the clinic—on a three count they collectively blew the candles out.

"You're not leaving the hospital already, are you?"

Theo pulled himself up short. He knew that commanding tone. And, of course, the accompanying blade of disappointment that made it cut deep.

"Dad? What are you doing here?"

"I want my stats checked."

"What? Why?" He glanced at his watch. He had a plane to catch. "We did your physical last month. There's nothing wrong with you."

"I want you to check again," Dimitri snapped, his eyes zigzagging round the reception area. "Or go get a doctor. One from the mainland. Stay. Then you can watch and learn."

He'd never stop, would he? Never stop belittling the choice Theo had made to be a GP.

Theo briskly guided his father to an exam table and yanked the curtain round them.

"I *am* a doctor," he said putting the blood pressure cuff on his father's wrist and briskly inflating it. "The last time I checked you were absolutely fine. Now, unless some strange new symptoms have presented themselves…" He stopped and looked at the results as the cuff peaked and deflated. "For a man who's been around the block a few times you are healthy as a horse. Happy, now?"

He hadn't spoken to his father like this since the day they'd gone to war about the clinic. He'd been filled with rage that again and again Dimitri had put barriers in the way of his living a life that was, at its heart, a good one. It might not be powerful. Or commanding. Or lucrative. But it was a good one. And *he* was a good man. And he was damned if Dimitri was going to stop him from fighting for the good woman who should be by his side.

His father was eyeing him, then he asked, "What kind of horse?"

Theo threw up his hands. "What the hell does it matter what kind of horse?"

Much to his shock, his father began to laugh. "Oh, Theo. You should see your face. You look—"

"What?" Theo was furious. "*What* do I look like?"

"You look just like me."

The thought sobered each of them. Of course it was impossible that they would physically resemble one another—but the rage, the hot flares of temper...those things were learned. And in that moment they both saw stark evidence that those lessons had in fact been handed from father to son.

"Dad…why are you here?"

"I heard you were leaving."

Theo would have asked how, but word always traveled fast around Mythelios.

"Yes. I'm going to see Cailey."

He braced himself for the inevitable explosion, the admonishment. The scorn.

Instead his father nodded, stared at his hands for a moment, then looked up into his son's eyes and asked in a cool, clear voice, "Would you like some money?"

Disbelief flared inside him with a white-hot rage. The protective walls he'd built round his heart came crashing down. Shame that he'd let Cailey return on her own swept through him, and just as quickly formed into an immovable rod of resolve.

"Is that how you plan on making your grandchild disappear? With money?"

His father looked at him, confused at first, and then pale as comprehension dawned.

"That's right, Dad. Your son has gone and done it again. Brought shame to the house of Nikolaides. What do you want to do this time? Try to pay me off to leave the island like you tried with Cailey?"

"No, I—" He reached out to Theo. "I thought we had an understanding."

"No, *you* had an understanding. I just agreed to it because, like a fool, I thought one day you'd see things the way I did. I thought you'd grow to like the clinic and see yourself as part of this community. But you still don't get it, do you?"

"What exactly am I meant to get?"

"That I am every bit the same as these so-called commoners. Flesh. Blood. With a heart beating in my chest that, no matter how much I try to deny it, has feelings. But I may as well face facts. No matter what I do, I'm never going to be enough for you."

"That's not true."

"Really? Where's the pride you should feel for me, Dad? We both know I'm not your true flesh and blood. That I didn't follow the path you wanted me to. I get it. I've been nothing more than a really expensive disappointment. Well, let's just call it quits now, shall we? What-ever it takes."

He was ranting now, but he couldn't stop himself. It was as if the floodgates had finally opened in his chest and there was no chance of closing them.

Unblinking, his father stared at him as he continued, "Shall we shut the doors of the clinic? You've done your bit. Seen the island through an earthquake. Your reputation will stay intact. We'll close it now and I'll spend the rest of my days working to pay back what you put into the clinic. Sell a kidney. Become the overpriced specialist you always dreamed of. And while we're at it why don't we dispense with the whole 'family' ruse? I'll address you as Dimitri, or Mr. Nikolaides, from here on out."

"What? No! I'm your *father*."

"Then why don't you ever act like one?"

They both stopped and stared at one another. Theo was shocked that he'd even asked. His father was pale.

Much to his amazement, his father sank onto a chair and dropped his face into his hands.

Theo fell to his knees, fearing his rage had gone too far, and pulled his father's hands away from his face. "Dad? Dad, are you all right?"

"I only wanted you to be happy."

Theo exhaled heavily. "I *am* happy. *Was* happy," he qualified. "This—" He spread his arms wide to show he meant the clinic. "This all made me very happy."

"Until *she* came back."

"Cailey? Yes. Cailey coming back made me even happier. It was when she went away that I realized what I'd lost." He sat back on his heels.

"Why did you threaten her ten years ago? Why did you make her leave the island?"

His father sat back wearily in the chair. "It is the only way I know how to do things. With power and money—the two things I never had as a boy. The same two things you never seemed to want."

"All I wanted was for you to love me."

"And I do."

"So…what? You show it by telling a girl from the wrong side of the tracks you'll put her mother and brothers out of work if she doesn't leave me alone?"

"I thought she would hold you back. That her…her learning difficulties, her desire to be here with her family, never to leave the island, would keep you from your dreams."

"*Your* dreams, you mean."

His father shrugged, then gave Theo a sad smile. "I think I got that part wrong."

"Yeah. You did. I truly love my job. I'm sorry I'm not what you wanted me to be, but this is what I love doing. And Cailey is the woman I should be jumping on a plane for and begging forgiveness from."

"What? Why do you need her forgiveness?" His father sat upright.

"I told her I didn't have it in me to be our child's father."

"Ridiculous. Of course you do. You're a Niko-laides."

Theo couldn't help but laugh. "That's exactly why I told her I didn't know if I had it in me."

Dimitri gave him a considering look for a long, uncomfortable minute, then abruptly shrugged the kind of Greek shrug that spoke a thousand words. It said, *You're right. I was wrong. You're my son. I love you. I support you.* It said all the things Theo had hoped to hear his whole life, and in one fell swoop gave him the belief that, although it was a tentative beginning, he and his father just might have begun a journey to heal a relationship that had never really had a chance to grow.

"Son…" His father grabbed hold of his arm and pulled himself up to stand. "When you get back from England…with Cailey…perhaps you can ask her to give an old man another chance."

"Perhaps you can ask her yourself."

"Perhaps I can." He nodded. Then lifted his blue eyes to his son in a swift move of impatience. "So, go." His father flicked his hands at Theo. "Go! Go and get this girl carrying my grandchild and come back soon. Your mother will be wanting to start knitting, or whatever it is grandmothers do."

Theo's expression turned sober. "I may not be successful in bringing her home, Dad."

"What? Don't be ridiculous." He clapped his son on the back. "You're a Nikolaides. You can do anything you set your heart on."

"From your lips—"

"I know, I know." His father looked upwards along with his son. "This one may be in the hands of the gods. But remember." He thumped his hand on his son's chest. "What you have in here is every bit as powerful."

Theo reached out and pressed the buzzer on the traditional English doorframe. Trust his sister to "go local."

Not that he'd expected to find a whitewashed, stone home with a blue door in the center of London, but… He turned and looked down the street and smiled. Black cast-iron gates. A perfectly manicured central square. People walking along the street avoiding eye contact. It was all so… *English*!

Then again, she'd never been one to do things by halves so why start now?

The door opened and an unexpected knot formed in his throat as his eyes lit on the sister he hadn't seen in far too long.

Was this proof he'd made the right decision?

"Theo?" Erianthe didn't bother hiding her astonishment and quickly threw her arms around him.

He folded his arms around her and enjoyed the unchecked emotion.

"Hey, sis," he murmured into her hair. "Fancy giving your old brother a bit of Dutch courage?"

A few minutes later, after his overnight case had been safely stored in the central hallway and his sister had plumbed a few key facts about his unexpected appearance from him, Erianthe handed him a strong cup of coffee.

"It's not exactly Dutch courage, but it'll have to do. No way am I sending you out on a mission this important with booze on your breath."

He grinned at his sister. She was so...*vital*! And focused. Everything about her spoke of the strength and determination she'd poured into the final years of her medical training as she honed in on her specialty. A far cry from the rebellious teen his father had shipped off to boarding school years ago.

"So!" Erianthe folded herself into an armchair across from the sofa where Theo had settled himself. "You've gone and got your teenage crush pregnant."

Theo whistled. "Don't bother mincing your words, will you, Eri?"

"No point," she parried. "Sounds to me like you've got a lot of making up to do. And if I know Cailey—"

"Have you seen her?" he interrupted, his heart skipping a beat.

"No." She shook her head. "I haven't seen her since I left Mythelios. Hey! Don't look at me like that. From what you've said, you didn't exactly stay in touch with her either. Not that you didn't make up for it during the quake." She laughed as only a kid sister could. With pure non-judgmental affection.

He nodded. "Fair is fair. I deserve your jibes...*and* hers."

"Oh, don't you worry." She batted away his concerns. "If she's anything like she used to be, I'm sure she'll let you know exactly how she feels."

Eri was right. Cailey had been nothing less than honest with him. And all he'd done was cloak himself in a protective shield of lies. Well, no more. Now that he'd begun to clear the air with his father he'd do his level best to be as honest and open with Cailey as he could.

He took a sip of the coffee and gave his sister a thoughtful look. "You've changed a lot since I saw you last."

She put her coffee cup down on the table beside her and traced a figure of eight on her knee. "It's easy enough to do when the motivation is right."

"What do you mean?"

She looked at him as if he'd asked the most inane question in the universe. "There was getting out from under Dad's thumb for one. Not letting him make decisions for me anymore. Proving his way of living life isn't the *only* way…" She raised her coffee cup to him in a "cheers" gesture. "Well done you, for getting the clinic built. I am still astonished he gave in."

Theo shifted in his chair. It hadn't been easy. But he'd stood up to his father and made his point. Now he needed to face his fears head-on.

Fears that he wouldn't be the father he knew his child deserved.

"You're wavering," Erianthe observed drily. "Stop wavering and start doing. Or, if you prefer, I can keep on reminding you about all of the lovely lessons our father taught us through the years."

She lifted her hand, as if in preparation to talk him through each point, and Theo laughed.

"I get it. Point made. Like I said, you've changed. And, believe it or not…he's beginning to as well."

Erianthe threw him a dubious look.

"Honest. He'll probably always be a crotchety, bull-headed businessman, but as a dad… He's trying. And that's something I have to learn from." His expression sobered as he looked across and met his sister's clear, intent gaze. "I want to be a good father."

"So?" She gave him a pointed look. "Why are you sitting here with me? Go out there, hail a taxi and get yourself over to the hospital—where I hope you'll drop to your knees and beg that girl to forgive you."

"That's your prescription?" He grinned and rose from his chair.

"As a doctor and a sister, yes." She smiled back at him and pushed him toward the door. "That's exactly my prescription."

CHAPTER SIXTEEN

"She's a real beauty."

Cailey smiled at the new father, his eyes misted over with the wonder of holding his daughter in his arms for the first time. Two weeks ago a moment like this would've sent her fleeing to the Ladies' to have a quiet little sob, but she'd had a stern talk with herself.

She'd worked in the maternity ward before she'd so much as had a boyfriend, let alone a chance at having a child of her own. Now she was perfectly placed to prepare for what lay ahead. Love, tears, pride. She'd seen all those things and more in the parents who had come through the ward, and she would continue to see them again and again.

Up until her own maternity leave, she thought, her hand giving the slightest hint of roundness on her belly a soft caress.

"I'd better get to the florists before they shut." The father reluctantly handed over the infant to Cailey. "Her mum deserves all the flowers in London for this. More."

Cailey gave his arm a rub with her free hand and spent a few moments cuddling the little girl after he'd left. It was a miracle, she thought. The gift of life.

"Just look at your little nose." She popped her index finger on its nose. "And your two tiny eyes. And two teeny hands… And one day you'll be all grown up."

"She's a real beauty."

Cailey started at hearing the exact same words she'd just heard coming from a very different voice. A voice she hadn't banked on hearing ever again.

Taking a moment to collect herself, she stroked the baby's cheek with the back of her hand, then gently placed it into its bassinet.

"Hello, Theo."

She resisted the urge to cross her arms over her chest to hide the pounding of her heart. "Are you here to see anyone in particular?"

Playing coy wasn't her usual remit, but she had to protect herself somehow. Why hadn't he just stayed away, as he had all but promised he would?

"I think I made some very serious mistakes recently."

"Oh?"

She swished past him and began walking toward the staffroom. Having this conversation, or *any* conversation, in front of these newborn babies felt like…treason or heresy or…*ugh*! She didn't know. It was hard to untangle one thought from the next, knowing the man she loved was doing his level best to catch up to her.

She whirled around and tumbled back a few steps when he nearly collided with her. Flailing for balance, she felt Theo's hands on her arms, steadying her.

She wrenched herself free. "Don't. Touch. Me."

"Cailey, please. I need to talk to you."

"Oh, really? Well, about two weeks ago I needed a father for my child. But we don't always get what we want, do we?"

The words hit their target. Theo looked as shocked as if he'd been hit by a car.

Her heart twisted against conflicting emotions. There was no pleasure in hurting him.

"I'm sorry." She took another step away from him. "I can't do this, Theo. Please, can you just go?"

"What if I said I was here to be that man?"

Her mind fuzzed. She'd built a wall around her heart over the past few weeks and in little less than the blink of an eye Theo had decimated it. She felt raw and exposed.

"You *aren't* that man," she choked out. "You told me as much."

"I said a lot of things," he agreed. "And most of them were about as wrong as they could be."

"Everything all right here, Cailey?" Elise appeared by her side. "I can call Security if you need me to."

Theo took a step back, his green eyes solidly on her own. "Ten minutes?" he begged. "Ten minutes…"

"Ten minutes for what?" asked Elise.

Cailey would have laughed if she hadn't been trying her best to control the jitters that had turned her nerves into a fistful of dancing crickets.

"To convince this beautiful woman to become my wife."

Elise's eyes widened. "Cailey Tomaras, you dark horse, you. Why didn't you tell me you were hiding this Adonis away in a corner?"

"He is a Theo, not an Adonis," she replied, instantly feeling her resistance wearing away.

His wife?

"Actually, I'm pretty busy," she said breathlessly.

She couldn't do this—melt at the first opportunity. It was what she'd done in Mythelios and look where that had landed her. Pregnant and alone.

Not. A. Chance.

"If you need medical help, sir, I think you will find A and E on the ground floor."

"Cailey."

Theo reached out for her hand and she pulled it away.

"Can we at least talk?"

"No." She pretended to look at a patient's form, but all she could see were blurry letters. She knew for a fact it wasn't her dyslexia this time. It was her body going into survival mode.

"Cailey, love." Elise took hold of both of her shoulders, dipped her head and looked her in the eye. "If you don't accept this man's proposal, d'you mind if I jump in there and accept for you?" She gave him a hungry scan then stage-whispered, "Just…*look* at him! Eye candy for life."

"Candy can give people cavities."

"And stress can give people ulcers," Elise retorted, completely immune to the simmering emotions roiling between Cailey and Theo.

"It's a good point." Theo adopted the manner of a wise old physician. "We wouldn't want stress hurting the baby, now, would we?"

"Baby!" Elise shrieked, and swiveled on Cailey. "You didn't tell me you were pregnant."

"I also didn't tell you that this big Greek meatball broke my heart."

Elise gasped and swatted at Theo's arm. "You scoundrel!" She stood next to Cailey and crossed her arms, clearly thrilled to be part of this living, breathing soap opera. "What did you do and how are you going to make up for it?"

"I didn't step up when I should have."

"Why not?" Elise was indignant.

"Because I was a fool. I was afraid I'd lose something I'd fought for, but now I realize absolutely nothing matters without Cailey in my life."

"Swoon!" Elsie did a dramatic dip of her knees and sent Cailey a look of sheer disbelief. "Why are you not throwing yourself into this man's arms?"

Cailey threw her friend a sidelong glance. However much she loved her bolshie attitude, this really was her battle to fight.

"Elise...do you mind if we have a few minutes alone?"

Elise looked between the pair of them, as if deciding whether or not there would be any danger in leaving them alone. "Right. I'll give you fifteen minutes in the on-call room and if I hear shouting I'm calling Security. If I hear nothing I'll presume you've made up and I'll put up the 'Do Not Disturb' notice. Are we clear?"

Cailey couldn't help but giggle at Theo's baffled expression. This was utterly ridiculous. Was he really here to try and win her hand in marriage?

She tipped her head toward the on-call room. "Fifteen minutes."

She drew in a deep breath, hoping it would give her the strength she'd need to say no regardless of whatever appeal he made. She'd made her decision. She wasn't prepared to endure any more heartache.

He could say what he needed to and then go home.

She was going to raise this child on her own.

The second the door closed behind them Theo took Cailey's hands in his. "I owe you an apology."

"You don't owe me anything."

"Yes, I do."

"What exactly is it you think you owe me?"

Theo looked her straight in the eye. "My respect, for one. I hadn't realized just how vile my father had been to you."

Cailey sucked in a sharp breath and pulled her hands out of Theo's. "I'm not here to talk about him."

"We have to."

"No 'we' don't. 'We' aren't a 'we.' You've made that very, very clear, Theo."

"I was wrong."

She shifted her jaw, almost as if she were chewing the words over. The admission hit her straight in the heart. She wanted to believe him. She really did. But there wasn't a chance she was going to let herself be dependent upon someone else's emotional or financial whims. Not with her child's welfare on the line.

"And what exactly does that mean for me?"

"It means I hope with all of my heart you will let me spend the rest of my life showing you just how much I respect you and honor you and cherish you."

"Those are all just words, Theo. They're worth about as much to me as the money in your father's bank account. Absolutely nothing."

Which, of course, was a lie. His words meant the world to her—but she couldn't show him that. Not with so much at stake. There wasn't a chance in the world she was going to open her heart to him again.

"Dad can't wait to meet his grandchild. He told me to tell you that."

Oh?

"You told him I was pregnant?"

That came as a surprise.

"Yes, I did. I also told him I was in love with

you. And that if he wanted the clinic he could have it."

Her eyebrows shot up.

Theo shot her a sheepish smile. "I did also offer to pay for it."

"How?"

"I haven't strictly worked that part out yet, but with you by my side I am convinced anything is possible."

"And how did Dimitri take this news? That you're willing to throw it all away for a housekeeper's daughter?" She narrowed her gaze. "Are you here because you've been banished, too?"

"No. Quite the opposite."

"Theo, if you're doing this just to put your conscience at rest, you can leave it—really. There are two things I learned about myself during the earthquake. The first is that I really love my job and I know I'm good at it. That gave me a sense of pride I've never really let myself feel before. And now that I have that I know I can be a perfectly good mother on my own. You made it explicitly clear you had no interest in following in your father's footsteps—"

"Which is why he and I had it out. Why I told him I needed to come here. Apologize. Win you back. I love you, Cailey Tomaras. With every cell in my body, I love you. And I am hoping you will do me the honor of being my wife."

"And the baby?" she asked softly.

"I *want* the baby. I've always wanted the baby. I just want to be good enough for it. And if you're willing to trust that I will do the very best I can we can make another baby after this one, and another after that one…"

Cailey giggled as she let him pull her to him. They kissed softly. Lovingly. Transferring the affection in their hearts into touches and caresses.

"What was the other thing you learned about yourself?" Theo asked.

"What? After the earthquake?"

"Mmm-hmm." Theo nuzzled into Cailey's neck, loving her scent, her touch.

"I learned how important family is. And how I'd really rather live in Mythelios than here in dreary old England."

Theo laughed. "I'm very happy to hear that."

"You are?"

He cupped her face in his hands and lowered his lips to hers. The kiss that followed embodied the perfection and timelessness of true love. Soft. Passionate. Tender. Powerful. She felt his love transfer directly to her heart, knowing that as each day passed it would only grow stronger and more resilient, no matter what life threw their way.

The sound of approaching footsteps halted their kissing. Through the doorway they heard Elise's muffled voice.

"It's been seventeen minutes. I'm putting the 'Do Not Disturb' sign on. You have half an hour. Start your watches!"

They stared at one another, then burst out laughing.

"Will you come back to Mythelios with me, Cailey?"

She nodded. "I will. But make me one promise."

"Anything," he said.

"I can work at the clinic."

"Done."

"Well, then…" She gave her watch a quick glimpse. "We've only got sixteen more minutes before I'm due back on. Fancy making good use of them?"

"It would be my pleasure."

CHAPTER SEVENTEEN

"WHAT ARE WE going to do?" Cailey was still staring at the monitor in disbelief.

"Build bunk beds, I guess." Theo laughed as he retraced the path of the monitor over his wife's gently rounded belly.

"Leda isn't going to take kindly to no longer being the Princess of the Cottage."

Cailey shot her husband a knowing look. Their daughter was glorious, but she had each of her parents wrapped firmly round her little finger.

"I suspect she shall take on the role of Queen with little prompting," Theo said, humor warming his voice like sun-drenched honey.

He handed his wife a few tissues to wipe the gel off her tummy after they'd spent a few more minutes gazing in wordless wonder at the new lives they had created.

Theo looked up at the wall clock. "We'd better get up to Mum and Dad's house soon."

"Lunch?"

Theo nodded, a wry smile on his lips. "Dad's got some new inflatables for the pool he wants to show off to Leda."

"He loves being a grandfather, doesn't he?" Cailey giggled. "What is it this time? A huge swan?"

"Flamingo," Theo answered. "He knows Leda loves pink."

"Can we stop by the *taverna* beforehand?"

"Why's that?"

Cailey slid off the exam table and shifted her top back into place. "I just thought perhaps we could let a certain someone know he might be a godfather soon."

Theo's eyes lit at the suggestion. "And that, my dear…" he crossed the room to give his wife a deep kiss "…is one of the many reasons why I love you."

She pulled back and smiled broadly, laughter rippling through her every word. "I *am* rather marvelous, aren't I?"

"The best," Theo answered without a moment's hesitation. "The absolute best."

* * * * *

Look out for the next story in the
HOT GREEK DOCS *quartet*

TEMPTED BY DR. PATERA
by Tina Beckett

And there are two more fabulous
stories to come!
Available July 2018!

If you enjoyed this story, check out these
other great reads from Annie O'Neil

REUNITED WITH HER PARISIAN SURGEON
HER KNIGHT UNDER THE MISTLETOE

Available now!